LOST
DOGS

Also by Garrett Carr

The Badness of Ballydog

LOST DOGS

GARRETT CARR

SIMON AND SCHUSTER

First published in Great Britain in 2010 by Simon and Schuster UK Ltd
A CBS COMPANY

The author wishes to acknowledge the assistance
of The Arts Council of Northern Ireland.

Simon & Schuster UK Ltd
1st Floor
222 Gray's Inn Road
London WC1X 8HB

This book is a work of fiction. Names, characters, places
and incidents are either the product of the author's imagination or
are used fictitiously. Any resemblance to actual people living
or dead, events or locales is entirely coincidental.

A CIP catalogue record for this book is
available from the British Library.

978-1-84738-599-4

1 3 5 7 9 10 8 6 4 2

Printed in the UK by CPI Cox & Wyman, Reading, Berkshire RG1 8EX

www.simonandschuster.co.uk

www.garrettcarr.net

1

He thought he was the last boy alive. He had not seen another person in four days, or was it six? Trapped in total darkness, he could not even see himself. He had to touch his eyelids to find out if his eyes were open. The food had run out. The boy survived by drinking rainwater running down the steel walls. His universe was pitch-dark and sealed tight. Sometimes, to remind himself he was alive, he shouted his own name.

'AKEEM!'

It echoed back off the walls.

There was only one dim star in Akeem's universe. A button was recessed in the wall above him. Its weak orange glow was his only comfort, but he knew never to push the button. That would be suicide, for it opened the freighter's forward door. The forward door was taller than Akeem, even though it was partly buried. It was cold to the touch. He ran his fingers along its watertight seals. Beyond the door was ocean, cold and vast.

Akeem prayed for London to be the freighter's destination. He was in its hold, a deep storage tank half full of coarse salt. High above his head, hatches were clamped down. The forward door was in the bow, ploughing through the sea. From the stern, through the bulkhead, came the muffled blare of the engine. It was loud but so steady that by the time he had spent a second day in the hold Akeem had stopped noticing it. The endless drone was just a new kind of silence. Akeem stayed by the forward door, dug into the salt. It had settled since leaving port, its level dropping by a metre. This salt was not the fine kind you put on food, it was unprocessed and gritty. But by the third day, barely aware of himself, Akeem was taking pinches of the salt and eating it. Hunger was as constant as the engine noise. It was a throb that underlay everything.

Akeem wanted to pray facing Mecca but had no idea of its direction. So the light of the button came to represent Mecca. He knelt before it. A Muslim is taught to pray five times a day but Akeem, under his breath, prayed much more than that. By the fourth day he was in a permanent state of prayer. Prayer was as constant as the engine noise, as constant as the hunger. Some boys, trapped and alone, would have felt forgotten by God. The closing of the hatches would have cut the cord to Him. But Akeem did not feel that way.

'Allah,' he repeated countless times, 'I am in the belly of this ship. Keep watch over me.'

Akeem was confident God was watching and would help him in his time of need. This was good. That time was coming.

Akeem woke with a start. It was the sixth day. He lay still a full minute before working out what had woken him. The note of the engine had dropped an octave. The freighter was gearing down. It had arrived.

'God is Great,' Akeem said.

He almost put in a request for London but decided it was too small an issue to bother God with now. There was a more immediate problem. It was every stowaway's problem immediately after arrival: getting off the freighter without being caught. Akeem was not free yet.

The hull gonged as it struck the quayside. The reverberation rang on and on, buzzing in Akeem's ears. Soon a crack appeared above his head. The hatches, hydraulics whining, drew back and hinged upwards, rising as two big triangles. Akeem expected blinding daylight, but instead stars twinkled in the gap. The cargo of salt picked up some light and gleamed softly. Akeem rubbed his eyes, looked, and rubbed them again.

'God is Great,' he said. His chance of escape was better under darkness. The rusty air began lifting. Akeem gulped fresh, warm oxygen. It tasted of a new life.

With a clank, the hatches locked into vertical position. Now Akeem could see there were ladders leading up out of the hold. Akeem moved towards the nearest. He knew that once he was halfway up he would be out of the shadows and exposed. He would have to be fast.

From the outside world came a loud iron grunt. Something was approaching from the sky. The arm of a crane swung into the frame of Akeem's view. A wrought-iron grabber, hung on steel cable loops, dangled from its end like a massive pendulum. The grabber was called a clamshell bucket, Akeem had seen the same kind of equipment at work before. Now the bucket was shut, like two hands cupped together. To Akeem, it seemed alive, so long had it been since he had seen a real living thing. A strange thought occurred to him, *did the human race die off while I was stowaway?* It was such an automated world that maybe crewless cargo ships sailed on to their destinations regardless. Hatches opened and cranes performed their duties automatically. After human extinction the machines rolled on.

But no. Crewmen were setting down the gangway. Akeem heard their shouts and recognised the thump and rattle as the gangway hit the quayside. He knew he would receive no kindness from the crew. On deck he would have to dash past them. They would have strong arms, well able to crush his ambitions.

Akeem inched towards the ladder.

On deck he would have to be wily, behave unexpectedly. He would not run for the gangway, he decided, but to the seaward side of the freighter, and dive.

Akeem was an excellent swimmer and not afraid of high dives. He had lived most of his life on the docks of Lagos. He and his friends had a money-earning performance for the passengers of big ferries. They canoed alongside as they docked. Passengers dropped coins close, but not too close, to the canoes. The boys were not meant to catch the coins in their hands, that would be too easy. They had to dive for them. This was the show. The coin would flicker as it descended, leaving a silvery trail of bubbles. Akeem would dive, his legs whipping tight together and driving him deep. Passengers watched the soles of his feet disappear into the blue. When Akeem re-emerged, the coin would shine in his raised hand.

That was when Akeem began thinking of the big boats as full of promise, possibility and coins. Where did they come from? Where did they go? Rich places. Places where he could live decently. Lisbon, Liverpool, London . . .

Above, the clamshell bucket had opened. There was the whirling sound of loosened winches. The bucket was not lowered. It was dropped. The whole freighter felt the blow and dipped in the water. The iron hands clamped shut, claiming a hillock of salt. Cables burned red-hot as the bucket retracted up, then swept out of view, an iron cloud raining loose salt. It pulled more stale air out of the hold after it. The fresh air of Akeem's future poured in.

I am so close, he thought.

But the ladder was so tall. The deck so wide.

The bucket swung back into view. Akeem had a new idea. It was dangerous, but as soon as he thought it he knew he would try it. Thinking it and trying it were the same thing.

As the bucket fell he dashed out to meet it. Air whistled down. The bucket blocked out the stars.

Too far. Back. BACK.

Akeem chucked himself backwards. The bucket hit the salt as if trying to knock a hole in the hull. Akeem smelled iron. He looked up at the bucket, twice his height, as it closed. It sealed itself into a resolute mouth. It was a straight mouth, not smiling, not frowning. It did not care either way.

Akeem jumped at it. His fingers dug into grooves in the ironwork. Winches whined and the bucket withdrew. Seconds, and it would be above deck level. If Akeem stayed clinging outside the bucket he would be seen. Besides, each fingertip was a focused point of pain. His hold was weakening. He had to get up. He had to get over. He had to get *inside* the bucket. But there was nothing to give leverage. Akeem was still dangling from the impenetrable bucket as it emerged from the hold. He glimpsed the new city. He saw tall buildings and mountains beyond. He saw the blinking lights of an aeroplane coming into land. He saw a motorway bearing a river of headlights. Then he let go.

Akeem hit the salt. On his back he watched the bucket rove away. Lying in the middle of the hold, Akeem was completely exposed. Black skin on a white landscape. But Akeem had a new idea. He did not move. He prayed.

'Allah,' he whispered. 'Let me keep my life. Let me keep my body. I will use them to honour you always.'

He was bargaining with God.

The bucket returned and Akeem was in the middle of its next drop, at least he hoped it was the middle. He curled himself up.

'Allah,' he said as air pressure squeezed his eardrums, 'let me keep my life—'

He bounced and the bucket was everywhere at once. He was spun in banks of salt. It compressed, crushing the air out of him and pinning his arms to his sides. The bucket was almost closed. Was his whole body inside? Akeem imagined the indifference of the bucket as it separated him from his feet.

'Let me keep my body—'

CLANG.

Akeem was still fully attached to himself and

encased in iron and salt. Lubricator smoked as the bucket raced upwards and away. When the crane's arm locked, the bucket swung back and forth a few times. Akeem was away from the freighter but now had a new worry.

'I will use it—'

A slit opened in front of Akeem's face. Again he saw city lights. The salt's clench fell away. He could move his feet again. Then his legs. Akeem took one longing look at the new city. He could see a lot from up there. He was obviously high up.

'. . . to honour you—'

He tried to think of it as a feet-first dive. Body straight, arms tight to sides.

'. . . always.'

He dropped.

Open.

Air.

Akeem struck the mouth of a new machine. He was flung along a curved trajectory and was in the salt again. He took a breath, his first in ten seconds. He was inside a funnel. Around him salt turned in a slug-gish whirlpool, disappearing down into itself and taking Akeem with it. From below he felt the tug of the inevitable. It was like being inside an egg timer.

Akeem bashed his chin as he was sucked through the centre. He fell through space before being embed-ded, up to his waist, in the peak of a salt cone. He was inside a warehouse now. No one around. Drips of blood fell from his chin. Akeem watched the red dots shine and expand on the white salt. After so much time in the dark the bright colour mesmerised him.

Right then Akeem was dazed. He should not have been watching colours. He should have gotten away from under the load about to be dumped on his head.

A column of salt hammered him down. He stayed still a few seconds. Blackness. No light. No air. *Am I dead?* The weight on his back increased. No, not dead, but buried. Now Akeem dug and kicked, trying to get out of the salt mountain. He imagined being buried alive, living but paralysed in its centre. He would die of suffocation if he was lucky. Or thirst if he was not.

The salt became denser around him. He fought for twenty seconds but was not out.

Which way am I going?

Forget Mecca, Akeem did not even know which way was *up*. He shoved some space out from around his face. A single hot terrified tear squeezed from his eye. It did not roll down his cheek. It rolled to the bridge of his nose and fell away from his face. Akeem realised he had been digging the wrong way, he was pointed down into the middle of the cone.

He dug sideways. Another bucket load was dropped. Akeem felt his ribs cracking. Suffocation, Akeem discovered, was the sensation of your lungs shrinking until they were like two dry tea bags. Soon he would be immobilised. Then doomed.

The bucket would work another hour. The freighter settled against the quayside. Once it had offloaded it would await its return cargo then go home. The salt cone filled one end of the warehouse, its base a perfect circle. The cone was pretty in a way, shimmering as it grew new layers. It was self-contained and peaceful, like a tomb. Then four fingers poked out.

It was like touching life itself. Akeem hauled himself out and rolled down the side. He crawled to a hiding place. He spat out salt, shook it from his ears and dug it from his hair. He thanked God again and again and again.

The funnel he had fallen through was a towering piece of equipment, going up through the warehouse roof. On its side were tall white letters: 'PORT OF HARDGLASS'.

'Hard . . . glass,' said Akeem.

It was not London but Akeem did not care. Maybe God had a plan for him in this city. He smiled. He had survived the journey and made it ashore. His arrival was blessed. It was fate. God was Great.

2

'Hold your horses a minute,' said May, 'till I finish this.'

While Akeem struggled ashore back at the quayside, May had an easier arrival on the other side of the city. Not that she felt lucky. She sent a text message from her mobile phone: 'Been here 10 minutes i hate it already'.

Sister Perpetua watched her from behind the big flat discs of her spectacles, her expression unreadable. 'Are you quite certain you're done?' she asked.

'Aye. Fire away.'

'Have you seen your room?' asked Sister Perpetua.

'It's hardly *me* room, is it?' said May. 'All the girls are squashed in there.'

May walked around, examining Sister Perpetua's chamber. Sister Perpetua was probably used to new students standing before her all submissive, heads bowed, but May did not respect people just because they had hung around long enough to get old. It was impossible to say how old Perpetua was. Ancient for sure, but not wrinkly. Instead of wrinkling she had dried out smoothly and evenly. She was tiny. Not much taller than May. Her spectacles overwhelmed her face. May was relieved to see that the nuns here wore ordinary clothes, not traditional gear. But this room! Who would paint a room grey? Holy statues and pictures were lined up everywhere. Jesus, Mary and Joseph, staring forlornly upwards or mournfully down. They never looked you in the eye, that lot. May went to the window. She was upstairs in a one-hundred-year-old farmhouse that was now a boarding school. It stood on the slope of a mountain, surrounded by trees. From the front door a gravel drive curved away. At the bottom an unnaturally steep embankment rose. Headlights shot along the ridge, pulsing as they passed through the treetops. The motorway led towards where an orange night-glow lit up the sky, the city of Hardglass.

Motorway traffic could be faintly heard inside the school. The dormitory was the former front parlour. It was packed with beds. Some were tall with brass fittings. The old farmer and his family had probably slept in them in their day, probably on the same mattresses. Other beds were flat-pack assemblages. Now seven girls were sleeping there. At the back of the house was a grand kitchen with massive porcelain sinks. Across the hall, the dining room also served as the classroom. Two tables were pushed together to make one long table. Every girl probably knew her own chair and would kill you if you sat in hers. Every chair was different. Everything about this place was mismatched. No floor was exactly even, no angle quite right. It was an ad-hoc school for all levels of academic ability. It also sheltered other unusual abilities. It was two nuns and, counting May, eight students. It was the Black Mountain School for Gifted Catholic Girls.

'This place is miles from the city,' complained May. 'I got friends there. I thought I'd be closer to the action.'

Sister Perpetua considered a while. 'Here at Black Mountain School,' she said eventually, 'we do not like action.'

May turned her back on Sister Perpetua again and looked out of the window. Car headlights were streaking towards the city.

'The other girls sound like a right bunch of saps,' said May.

May did not see Sister Perpetua's lips quiver in anger. A second later they resolved back into a neutral line on her face. The nun contemplated a candle flame.

'Many of the girls have had difficult childhoods,' said Sister Perpetua. 'The secluded atmosphere of Black Mountain School is good for them. It may even be good for you. I understand you also have experienced neglect.'

May snapped around and looked at the nun. Sister Perpetua's head was angled to one side. The angle of her head seemed to say: *we have seen your type before.*

I will hate her, May decided.

'So,' said Sister Perpetua as she sat back in her chair, 'tell me about your Gift.'

May made a bored sound. 'I already told that other nun when she visited me,' she said.

'Now tell *me*,' said Sister Perpetua. 'Is your Gift telling you anything at the moment?'

'It never shuts up,' said May. It was true. It was like a constant whisper in her mind. It was sometimes overpowering but recently May had been honing her ability. She was learning to tune in and out of the animals in her environment according to her own will.

'Ye've got mice,' said May.

'Anything else?' said Sister Perpetua.

The moment May arrived she had felt a strong mentality. It was coming from behind the school. It knew the thrill of open country and the firm hand of Sister Perpetua.

'A horse,' said May.

'Correct,' said Sister Perpetua. 'I've a stable out the back. Gender?'

'Boy,' said May. 'The only boy ye ever let near this place, I'd say.'

Sister Perpetua pressed on. 'His name is Saint. What's he doing now?'

May paused long enough to show Perpetua she was doing her a favour. Then she closed her eyes and opened her mind.

'He's sleeping, dreaming.'

Sister Perpetua could not hide her interest. She leaned forwards, putting her elbows on her knees. 'What does he dream of?' she asked.

'Same thing horses always dream of,' said May, eyes open again. 'How beautiful they are. Horses are completely hung up on themselves. They're arrogant.'

'So, you can recognise arrogance in others,' said Sister Perpetua, 'that, at least, is a start. Is Saint dreaming of anything else?'

It was true that Saint was vain. But he was also dreaming of Sister Perpetua, her fingers in his mane and her calming voice in his ear.

'No, that's it,' said May.

Disappointed, Sister Perpetua sank back in her chair. 'You've had a long day,' she said, 'you'll want to go to bed.'

Actually, May wanted to be in one of those cars heading for the city. Her friends Ewan and Andrew were in Hardglass, so near but yet so far. In the black reflection of the window May watched Perpetua rise from her chair. The nun stood behind her, using the dark reflection to study her newest student. For a horrible moment May thought the nun was going to put a hand on her shoulder.

Instead she said, 'Your Gift is humbling. It is evidence of God's grace. But I believe, with hard work, faith and focus, we can build on it. We will begin a regime of training. Currently, you can only *receive* from animals. But you're going to learn to reach back to them.'

May could not believe she had actually *wanted* to come to this place. Now she was being forced into a regime of training. What could Perpetua understand of her ability? Already May hated this sheltered atmosphere. This madhouse of nuns and fragile girls. This complete nightmare.

May was fourteen years old, and angry.

3

Andrew was dazzled. The supermarket was bright as a small sun. Its glass façade rose above the car park. He wondered how much electricity the supermarket burned, say twenty thousand watts on light? Then add refrigeration. Then automatic doors and chiming cash registers. The mathematics soon got beyond Andrew's reach. Hundreds of fluorescent tubes radiated white light. The supermarket seemed weightless. Like it might have snapped its moorings and floated into outer space. Maybe that was where it came from. A gift from the future.

Andrew did not like the city's excess. Kilfeather's small shop back home was enough for him.

He was in the back seat of a car. Ewan's mother was in the front. Ewan had gone into the supermarket with Officer Jones. Stirling was out of his driver's seat and standing a few metres away, smoking a pipe and watching. Stirling was plain-clothed, like his partner, but Andrew knew he was armed.

The trial of Ewan's father was beginning the next day and was due to last a few weeks. It was hoped that Ewan's mother's testimony might help free him. For the last six months she and her son had been hidden in Andrew's and May's hometown, to hide them from 'rogue elements' who might have different ideas. Ewan's father stood accused of dealing weapons. There had been plenty of buyers. Hardglass had been a battleground for a long time but the badness was behind it now. There had been a ceasefire and years of negotiations. The Peace Process had taken over.

What am I doing here? he wondered.

But he knew the answer. Andrew was there because he had made a promise. He made the promise because it *seemed* like the right thing to do but Andrew was new to this. He was not always sure what the right thing was. There were no guidelines. The Green Cross Code, the Ten Commandments, nothing came close to covering all the situations a teenager faced.

Was honesty right?

Sometimes honesty was cruel.

At first Andrew had invented reasons why he could not leave his hometown. That did not stop Ewan's mother pestering him. She even offered to pay him cash. Now he was looking at the back of her head. Even from here she looked stressed.

Was pity right?

Pitying someone can be close to despising them.

It was pity, not money, that made Andrew promise to 'take care of Ewan'. He felt sorry for Ewan's mother. Keeping a promise was definitely *right*, Andrew had no doubt about that. When you got old everything was open to exception. Andrew thought no adult took a promise as seriously as even a young child could. He thought older people were basically washed-out versions of their younger selves. Ewan's mother, for example, seemed to have given up on everything. He pitied her.

'Thanks again for coming with us,' she said, looking back at Andrew. 'It'll be good to know you're keeping Ewan out of trouble while I am in court.'

Andrew shrugged. 'No problem,' he said.

What kind of trouble would Ewan get into anyway? He just liked reading books and watching telly. Andrew was the one who got into trouble. Or used to, anyway.

Andrew looked across the car park to make sure Ewan was not yet returning. He wanted some honesty. He did not care if it was cruel. 'Do you really think you should be defending your husband in court?' he asked.

No reply. Her tired shoulders drooped further.

'Ewan is pleased and proud and all that,' Andrew added. 'It's just from what I've heard your husband sounds . . . guilty.'

19

'You want to know how it is for *me*?' Ewan's mother said eventually. She was irritated and did not look around. 'All right, but you won't like it. Ewan is loyal to his father. He thinks *I* am loyal to him too.' She glanced across the car park just as Andrew had. 'But I am not.'

Andrew tried to take it in. 'You mean you're not going to defend him?' he asked.

'No, I am not a defence witness,' she said. 'The police made me see the harm that man has done. Ewan doesn't know. Not yet. I want you here if he finds out.' She paused and rephrased, '*When* he finds out.'

'Hang on, you're a witness against your husband?'

'I am *the* witness against him.'

Things made more sense now. She was constantly buying the best stuff for Ewan. She bought Andrew and May mobile phones too, so they could all stay in touch. Ewan's mother was buying love to cash in later. The boy had everything, except a mother who wanted to keep his father from prison.

Andrew was fourteen years old, and just wanted to do the right thing.

4

Ewan wanted to demonstrate his intelligence. He studied the supermarket's display of DVDs like he was a professor and they were important Latin texts. He watched Jones from the corner of his eye. Officer Jones had regularly visited Ewan and his mother while they were in witness protection. Ewan always looked forward to her visits. Now she was further down the aisle, looking at the covers of celebrity magazines. Ewan hoped she was only passing the time, not really interested in that kind of trash. How old was Jones? Perhaps twenty-nine, thirty, or some other far-flung number. Was she Catholic or Protestant? Ewan did not care. The old divisions were a thing of the past.

Ewan turned back to the DVDs. There were lots of *CSI* and *24*. He would not buy them. They were not intelligent. Besides, he had seen most of them already. Now he was seeking a nature documentary, although Ewan thought nature documentaries and crime dramas actually had a lot in common. Both were basically about survival. Survival in the green jungles of nature or in the concrete jungles of big cities. In both you knew there would be predators and wary innocents. You knew there would be chases and tactics. You knew not everyone was going to live.

'Look at this lot,' laughed Jones as Ewan approached. With a wave of the hand she dismissed the brash magazines, the heartbreaks, shock confessions and love triangles. 'I mean: who cares?'

'I knew you weren't interested in them,' Ewan sighed.

Jones grinned. Droopy eyelids gave her a permanently sardonic expression. She was tall; gangly some would say. She was not as pretty as the girls on the covers of the magazines. But to Ewan she was.

Crowds of shoppers pushed along the aisles. Their eyes darted about the bright product displays like fish moving along tropical reefs. Ewan and Jones weaved between trolleys. 'Peace in Hardglass at last . . .' said Jones sarcastically. 'Let's go shopping!'

Checkout counters went on forever in both directions. It was as if two giant mirrors faced each other, creating an infinity between them. But there were no mirrors, just a lot of checkouts. Ewan and Jones filtered through, paid, and were extruded onto the car park.

'Done?' Stirling asked, looking at his watch, as they approached the car.

Jones grinned. 'Oh, take it easy,' she said. 'Look, I

bought you an apple.' She pressed the apple in his hand. They all got in the neutrally coloured car. Jones sat between the two boys in the back. Stirling got behind the wheel and buckled his seat belt.

'Stirling never eats chocolate or anything *wild* like that,' said Jones. 'He only likes sensible, healthy, round-shaped things.'

Everyone smiled. Stirling too, it was all he could do. Stirling was not good with quick retorts. Instead he started the engine and said, 'As we've deviated from protocol and spent time in public we'll drive around a while before going to the Witness House.'

'Just a precaution,' explained Jones.

The motorway swept over rooftops. Cruising it felt like flying. Ewan watched rows of houses glide by, each going its own speed depending how far away it was. Countless houses of red brick, each with trim gardens and new extensions. Each front window flickered by the light of a widescreen television. Street lights ensured against shadows. The whole place hummed with electric contentment.

The motorway passed close over the street Ewan grew up on. He turned in his seat and watched it recede. Determinedly, his mother kept her eyes on the road ahead. They were not going home. They were going to the Witness House. It was a secret dwelling kept by the Justice Department for witnesses like her. They slipped into the anonymous suburbs.

'You got some animal shows?' she asked, looking back at Ewan. She was trying to be nice but Ewan lurched internally. *Does she have to talk like that? In front of Jones?*

'Natural history documentaries, yes,' said Ewan.

They seemed to drive down the same street three or four times. Was Stirling making sure they were not being followed or did every street just look the same? Ewan noted a name, Oak Street, to see if they came back this way.

'Now,' said Jones. 'Your mam will have a tough day tomorrow. It would be good to keep her company in the evening when she gets back, hmm?'

'Sure,' said Andrew.

'I want to go and visit my father,' said Ewan.

'There'll be plenty of time to catch up later,' Stirling advised.

'Best to let him and your mam focus on the trial first,' added Jones.

'Why does my mother have to be there the first day?' asked Ewan.

'Because she's the first witness,' Jones replied.

This got Ewan thinking. He was not certain that things learned from American crime dramas could be applied to Hardglass courts. But what was there to defend against until after accusations were made? Witnesses for the prosecution were called first, witnesses for the defence second. It was logical.

'Don't prosecution witnesses always take the stand first?' he asked.

'Well— I mean, there are exceptions . . .'

Jones soon sank into a swamp of contradictions. Ewan watched Stirling's fingers squeezing the steering wheel. He recalled a dozen other awkward conversations. Now they clicked into place. He realised what was going on. His mother was not going to defend his father. She was going to have him locked up.

'You can stop now.' Ewan's mother stopped Jones's stammered explanations. 'He was bound to work it out sooner or later.'

Ewan was fourteen years old, and had just demonstrated his intelligence.

5

Next morning May awoke completely under her blankets, both hands wrapped around her mobile phone. She stretched her legs towards the foot of the bed. The sheets parted like stiff paper. She listened. The worry of mice wafted from beneath the floorboards. Mice, May knew, lived always in a state of anxiety. Then she heard someone getting out of bed.

Lizzy Gamble was up. A minute later the alarm clock radio went off. Pop music blared, too big for the speaker. Sally Green sat up and turned down the volume. She performed a stretch and loud yawn, full of positivity for the day. Mona Longley turned and buried her face in her pillow. It muffled a tortured sigh. Tara Lyttle grunted, kicked off her blankets, stomped to the foot of her bed and snapped her bedclothes smooth. But at Elizabeth Dovell's bedside she behaved differently. With care, she brushed hair back from Elizabeth's face. Rafferty helped her lift Elizabeth into her wheelchair. Sally Green supervised. Rosy

Motherwell ambled back and forth in pink pyjamas. 'I'll put the kettle on for tea,' she said. Then she stopped at the foot of May's bed and studied the lump in the blankets.

May pretended to sleep. The previous night she had crept into the dormitory without meeting or waking anyone. From under her blankets she now listened to the students prepare for school or chores or whatever they did here. There was laughter, minor squabbles and things borrowed and returned. The racket died down but the girls had not left the dormitory. May sensed them standing around her.

'Time to get up,' a voice said.

Only one way to face so many new people at once: fast. May whipped off her blankets and sat bolt upright. 'I slept in,' she said.

Seven girls were looking at May. May looked back at them.

'Welcome to the Black Mountain School for Gifted Girls,' said an overweight student. 'My name is Rosy.'

'I'm May.'

'I knew that,' announced a girl with hair tied back tightly. 'I looked at your report. I do secretarial work for Sister Perpetua. I'm Sally Green.'

All the girls were around May's age apart from two who were only nine or ten. A girl with long straight black hair was on the bed next to May's. She had obviously got up, dressed, put on purple eye shadow and

27

then, to keep the day at bay, wrapped herself back in a blanket. Her chin and nose were so pointy she made you think of triangles. She did not look May in the eye. Instead she focused on her shoulder. 'Do you like *The Pixies*?' she asked.

May shrugged. 'Don't know,' she said.

One of the young ones spoke. 'That's Mona and I'm Rafferty,' she said. 'I used to have a first name but I dropped it, along with my old life, when I joined Black Mountain. I don't know if you want to fit in with us weirdos, but if you do we're happy to have you.'

'Aye, all right,' said May. 'Thanks.'

A girl with big eyebrows pushed a wheelchair to May's bedside. 'This is Elizabeth,' she said gruffly, referring to the girl in the wheelchair. 'She's the most Gifted of all of us.'

Elizabeth was smiling but not for May. Her smile was permanently set. Elizabeth never blinked. She saw nothing and everything at the same time. Her head was crooked down on one shoulder and her forearms were angled rigidly upwards to where her hands were making abstract shapes in the air. A trickle of drool oozed down her chin.

'She is a channel for God's love,' said Rafferty.

'The purest love,' said Rosy solemnly.

'Yadda yadda,' yawned Mona.

The grumpy girl snorted at Mona and reversed

Elizabeth away. 'Better get up,' she told May over her shoulder. 'This isn't a holiday camp.'

'That's Tara,' said Rosy as May got out of bed. 'You get used to her.'

Sister Primrose fluttered into the dormitory. 'Breakfast, breakfast,' she said. She hovered about, smoothing out beds, fixing hair, encouraging the doubtful and generally patting everyone towards the door. Sister Primrose was nervous and shy. She had grown up on a remote farm. Her childhood friends had been the clouds and the trees. Like a bird flitting from branch to branch, Sister Primrose approached May indirectly. May watched her warily. Suddenly Primrose's arms were wrapped around May and hugging her tight.

'Everything will be fine,' she whispered in May's ear. 'We're going to take care of you.'

May's arms hung stiff by her sides. Was she supposed to hug back? May did not have a mother. She was not used to this maternal carry-on.

At the head of the table, Sister Perpetua's seat was empty. Rosy gave May a seat between her and Mona. Some girls called this room the dining room and some called it the classroom, as lessons were conducted here also. It depended, May supposed, on what was most important to them, classes or food. Sally and Rafferty called it the classroom. Mona called it the dining room. May decided to call it the dining room too.

Breakfast was porridge. The girls laughed when May admitted she had never eaten it before.

'We take turns in the kitchen,' said Sally. 'You'll learn to make porridge soon enough.'

Until now her grandma was the only person May knew with the Talents. Now here were seven girls with Talents, all at once. May thought they would all want to show off their abilities. She certainly did. But instead nobody even mentioned them. May looked out at ravens flying the blue sky. Between the windows was a statue of some saint or another. It seemed to May there were dozens of holy statues around here, armies of Joseph, legions of Mary.

Tara came from the kitchen, spinning a tray of bowls. She banged one down in front of everybody. Tea was poured but Lizzy was confused. Instead of pouring milk in her tea she poured it on the tabletop. Sister Primrose wiped it up while whispering to Lizzy reassuringly. May could not help but stare.

'Lizzy's totally weird, isn't she?' said Mona, in a tone of I-know-why-and-you-don't. Mona was a bit weird herself. She never looked anyone in the eye and she dressed like a vampire. May knew that kind of gear was fashionable in some places. She had seen MTV, once.

Out of the blue Lizzy said, 'Good morning, Sister Perpetua.'

Sister Perpetua was not in the room.

The foremost smell was buttered toast. The foremost sounds were talking and spoons hitting bowls, clatter and chatter. Sugar and pots of jam were passed hand to hand or sent skimming across the table. Everything stopped as Sister Perpetua entered and walked the length of the room.

'Good morning, girls,' she said.

'Good morning, Sister Perpetua,' the students sang in unison.

Sister Perpetua took her seat. Sally had arranged her breakfast, black tea and two pieces of dry toast. Sister Perpetua gave the impression of having already been awake for hours. She looked at everyone from behind her spectacles. 'Let us pray,' she said.

The girls clasped their hands together and looked towards heaven. Mona rolled her eyes. May looked at the ravens.

'So,' said Sister Perpetua afterwards, 'our family has a new member. We thank God for her.'

There was a murmur of assent. After prayers the atmosphere was formal.

'May has a Gift I always thought could exist,' continued Sister Perpetua. 'She has a special bond with God's fauna. Isn't that beautiful?'

There was quiet around the table as the girls contemplated this.

'You read animal's minds?' inquired Rosy politely, maybe just to fill the silence.

'More like I'm able to feel what's passing through them,' said May. 'I tune in to them. Sometimes, if there're loads of animals around, it's a big racket in me head.'

More silence.

'It's not a bad thing,' May added quickly. 'I like it.'

'Now, who would like to be first to tell May about their Gift?' said Sister Primrose.

No one. Most of the girls looked down, afraid of being chosen. Even Sally Green pretended to be fascinated by her cutlery.

Dutifully, Rosy broke the silence. 'I detect illnesses in people,' she said. 'I see it in their aura.'

'Rosy uses her Gift for the benefit of others,' said Sister Perpetua. 'She frequently visits hospitals in the city and helps doctors with their diagnoses.'

'She's a real supa-dupa superhero,' said Mona.

'Now, Mona,' said Sister Primrose. 'Be nice.'

Sister Perpetua took off her spectacles and wiped the round lenses. Her eyes were sunken and small. 'Of course, Rosy's Gift is especially suited to aiding her fellows,' she said. 'But so can all your Gifts. It's just that some of their uses are less obvious.'

'Doctors know about your Talent then?' May asked Rosy.

'A few do.'

'And some police detectives know about Sally, isn't that right?' said Sister Perpetua, looking at Sally, requiring her to speak.

'I feel where bad things have happened,' explained Sally unwillingly. 'Murders especially. It's like a rip in the ground only I can see ... I'm good at finding bodies ...'

Sister Perpetua took over. 'As you know, May, before the Peace Process we went through years of conflict here. With her Gift, Sally has found the unmarked graves of some victims. This can bring a little comfort to their families.'

Sally was examining her cutlery again. May felt sorry for her. No wonder these girls were not excited about their Talents. Their Talents were duties.

May looked to Mona but Mona pretended not to notice.

'Mona keeps her Gift secret,' said Rosy, seeing what May was thinking. 'She never tells anyone.'

'We're sure she must have a Gift though,' laughed Rafferty, 'being as she's not afraid of us.'

'Our Rafferty looks about nine years of age,' said Sally, as if in compensation. 'But she's not. Rafferty grows amazingly slow. Actually she's sixteen years old.'

Rafferty made a wavering motion with one hand. Sixteen was only her approximate age. She had abandoned her past more than once. With nobody to guide her and a history of care homes and running away, Rafferty had lost count of her years.

'Think of all Rafferty will be able to learn in her long

33

life,' said Sister Perpetua. 'And all she will be able to teach.'

May was getting more and more annoyed with Perpetua's *wisdom*.

'Lizzy is . . . highly unique,' said Sister Primrose, choosing her words carefully. 'You might have noticed she is a bit *removed*. She lives in the future. Not by much. Only a minute or so, but this means she has difficulty relating to people around her.'

'She's able to see the future?' asked May.

'More than see it,' said Rosy, 'she's already in it.'

May was stunned. Lizzy was a minute ahead on the timeline? It boggled the mind, but did explain a few things.

'It is possible to speak with her,' said Sister Primrose, 'but not easy.'

'I'm best at it,' said Sally, perking up again. 'You concentrate real hard and tell yourself that you're *going* to say something to Lizzy in a minute. Then she'll reply. The head-melting part is: when the minute passes you *don't* have to actually say what you'd planned.'

'Which teaches us something,' said Sister Perpetua. 'The future is not written in stone. That lesson is Lizzy's Gift to us.'

Sister Perpetua found morals in everything, but May thought Lizzy's condition was depressing. Lizzy was only ten years old. Her time-bubble would always isolate her. Then there was Elizabeth, her body was a prison, further bound in a wheelchair. It was obvious Elizabeth could not talk, so May's eyes passed over her and on to Tara. Tara was concentrating hard on not being asked. She stared resolutely at the tabletop. 'I don't want to talk about it,' she announced.

'Now, Tara,' said Sister Primrose. 'You're getting so good at controlling it.'

Tara stared up at May hatefully, as if this was all her fault. Then May's bowl hopped an inch in the air and landed with a thud. May gasped. Nothing had lifted it. Nothing had gone near it. She looked up at Tara but she had turned away. The bowl was Tara's statement. She would say no more.

'Ye all call them Gifts,' May said to everyone. 'I call them Talents.'

'We'd noticed that,' said Sister Primrose, glancing at Sister Perpetua.

'Nobody gave me this ability,' said May. 'I learned to handle it alone. Most of me life I didn't even want it. I feared it. I learned for meself that it's the best thing I got.'

'You need humility before God,' said Sister Primrose. 'It's a Gift and He gave it to you.'

'No, it's mine. I earned it.'

'You're not done earning yet,' said Rafferty. 'You might never be.' It was strange getting stern advice from a nine-year-old, whatever age she really was.

'Not much of a Gift then, is it?' said May. 'If God hangs about to see if ye get to keep it. No wonder you're all depressed. Ye've no pride in what ye can do.'

'We're not depressed,' objected Sally. 'We're just aware of our responsibilities.'

'The "Talent" verses "Gift" debate is certainly interesting,' said Sister Perpetua evenly. When she spoke everyone listened. 'They're only words, and not such different words. Yet, calling your ability a Gift or a Talent does say a lot about how you could use it. *Gift* implies your ability comes straight from God. It means you should be grateful. It may also mean your ability is not entirely yours. You should use it to help humankind.'

She paused and contemplated May's defiant face.

'Like Spiderman becoming a crime fighter,' offered Mona quietly.

'Yes, Mona,' said Sister Perpetua without taking her lenses off May. 'Like Spiderman becoming a crime fighter.'

Sister Perpetua continued, '*Talent*, on the other hand, suggests your ability is born of you. You don't owe anything. You are your own divinity. There may not even be a God at all. They're an interesting contrast: Talent and Gift.'

Sister Perpetua looked out of the window, up to the ridge of Black Mountain. She appeared to be considering the choice between the two words but everyone knew she was not. Her mind was made up decades ago. It was a matter of faith.

Sister Perpetua turned back to May. 'Here we call them Gifts,' she said.

The girls bowed their heads, feeling May's chastisement as if it was their own. Nervously, Rosy took a mouthful of cold tea. They knew Sister Perpetua spent hours meditating in her chamber. She was enlightened. Her word was final. They could not believe it when May spoke back.

'Ye lot call them what ye like, I'll call them Talents,' she said. 'It's got nothing to do with God. We're straight from nature. Girls like us are older than religion.'

Sally's voice was pitched high in shock and disgust, 'How'd you explain that only Catholics are born with the Gifts then?'

Rosy spluttered on her tea.

'It's crazy-talk saying only Catholics get the Talents,' said May. 'I can't believe, with this Peace Process and all, that there are still schools separated by religion like this one. I'd say there's been girls like us for a million years. We're as old as the world.'

Sister Perpetua stood. 'May,' she said, 'a talk in my chamber, I think.'

6

The guard by the scanner shook his head in apology. 'No unaccompanied minors,' he said.

'I am sixteen,' said Ewan. He spoke flatly, to discourage debate, and looked the guard steadily in the eye. Ewan was not used to lying. But he could learn.

The guard sucked air through his teeth. He did not believe him. The boy actually looked about twelve, with his innocent face and wide curious eyes, but he also looked serious. Like he had a tonne weight on his shoulders.

'Put any metal objects in the tray then so,' said the guard, casting his eyes away in acquiescence.

Outside, summer sun was warming the pavements, but the detention centre was a half-buried bunker shunning the world. Air was forced in with pumps. In the old days of terrorist attacks and rioting, lots of buildings in Hardglass had looked like this, blocky and suspicious, pockmarked with small windows that would not shatter in a bomb blast. Now, hunched between soaring glass office blocks, the detention centre seemed stunted and dull-minded. Inside, the chemical light made Ewan notice his veins. From side tunnels came the sound of clashing gates and the prickly smell of frustration. This was the real meaning of *detention*.

The floor, the walls and even the roof of the visitors' room were covered in white tiles. They reflected the light intensely enough to sting. A bored guard stood at the back, a hoop of swipe cards hanging from his belt. The tables and chairs were of thick moulded plastic, designed to be easy to clean and difficult to smash over heads. Ewan's father stood as he approached. Despite the surroundings, Ewan had the feeling of returning home, of coming into dock. His father's teeth flashed, reflecting the tiles. His name was Franklin.

Franklin extended his hand and Ewan's hand disappeared into it. They shook. Physical contact was not allowed. The guard shuffled but did not intervene.

'Well, well,' said Franklin, still smiling, 'have a seat and tell me about the big bad world.' He leaned back to get a better view of his son.

'I only just found out she's against you,' said Ewan.

'A shock, eh?' said Franklin. 'But don't be too hard on your mam. I put her through a lot. She was my first love and she'll be my last.'

'Is it true . . . what they say?'

Franklin raised his eyebrows. This was to suggest he

39

did not understand Ewan's vague question. Franklin wanted to ascertain how much he had to admit to. He would admit to that and no more. Franklin was good at controlling the flow of information.

Ewan clarified. 'True that you sold weapons?'

Franklin made a long sigh. 'There never was much money in importing shoes. That school you went to, that posh house we lived in, how'd you suppose I paid for all that, eh?'

That was a *yes*, Ewan supposed, or as close as he would get. Perhaps, to his father, weapons were only another type of import. Ewan remembered that their dinner-time conversations had often focused on trade, on investment and return. Ewan had never liked these subjects. He would retreat to his room and watch television.

'You helped make the war,' said Ewan.

'The war was happening anyway,' said Franklin, folding his arms. 'There always was war, there always will be and people have the right to defend themselves. When companies make and sell weapons, it's called legitimate business. When an individual entrepreneur does it, it's called crime.'

Franklin stopped and lifted his hands in gesture of futility. Ewan turned away.

'We could cry about it,' Franklin said to him, 'but I'd rather put it behind us and do something useful for the Peace Process instead.'

'Like what?' Ewan asked, looking back. He was eager to hear anything to make his father seem a better person.

'I can't talk to you about that.'

Ewan's face fell.

'Maybe in a while, eh?' Franklin said, before bluntly changing the subject. 'Who's taking care of Blondie while I'm in here? My sister?'

Ewan nodded. 'I'll take care of her for you if you'd rather.'

Franklin savoured his son's loyalty. 'I've missed you,' he said. 'And your mother too, despite it all. Does she still wear our wedding ring?'

'No,' said Ewan, 'although she still has it. I thought she'd stopped wearing it so people wouldn't ask where you were.'

Franklin watched him. He was calculating risks, potential profit and loss. Other inmates were led towards their visitors. They wore blue one-piece uniforms, unlike Franklin who was ready for trial in a shirt and tie. When they had passed, Franklin spoke again. 'Don't look so sad,' he said. 'You want to know what I'm doing for the peace, eh? I probably shouldn't tell but you can handle it. You always were smarter than average. You got in to visit me alone. You're something special.'

Franklin laughed. Ewan smiled for the first time since discovering his mother's treachery.

'For the Peace Process all armed groups in Hard-glass are busy putting their weapons "beyond use",' Franklin explained, leaning in and speaking in a near-whisper. 'In plain English that means smashing the weapons, melting them down, or sinking them in concrete. But I sold special weapons. *Strange* weapons. The people who bought them aren't finding it easy to destroy them. So I'm helping. I'm having them all collected and brought to a warehouse in the docks that I have rented. Once they're all there I'll get rid of them myself. The country will be free of them.'

'How can you get rid of anything?' whispered Ewan. 'You're in here.'

'Magee represents me on the outside. Do you remember him? With the eyepatch? We communicate by mobile.'

'From in here?' asked Ewan, glancing at the guard.

'They won't take the mobile off me,' Franklin said. He indicated back at the guard with his head but did not mean just him, he meant the entire system. 'They're the ones gave it to me. The whole country wants rid of those weapons. They're letting me make my arrangements. Mind you, I don't get loud with the phone. It's only for text messages.'

'Will getting rid of the weapons help your trial?'

'It's not admissible,' said Franklin, sitting back and returning to his normal level of voice. 'It doesn't change history.'

'You're doing it out of the goodness of your heart?' Ewan was confused.

'My heart,' laughed Franklin, 'is an old grey thing . . . let's say I'm doing it for your mother. Is that an explanation?'

Ewan's expression was flat as a plate. He waited. He could also control the flow of information.

'It doesn't make sense, I know,' continued Franklin, 'but you're smart enough to know that sometimes life doesn't make sense.'

More visits were happening by now. The visitors were all women with young children. Prams were parked around the room. The air was full of tears and hissed, disappointed conversations.

'I've to go now,' said Franklin, looking towards his exit. 'It's the opening arguments.'

'I am not allowed in court,' said Ewan.

'That suits me,' said Franklin. 'I prefer you don't hear all that. I'm looking forward to seeing your mother though.' Franklin laughed, then leaned close again, his arms on the table. 'Will you do something for me?' he asked.

Ewan waited.

'Bring me our wedding ring. If you don't want to I'll understand. But your mother's not wearing it, is she? It'll be a kind of token for me. If I have a heart it's in that ring.'

Ewan looked away, avoiding his father's gaze. Everywhere he looked, white tiles glinted.

Franklin sat back. 'If it's too much to ask—'

'No,' said Ewan quickly, 'I'll try.'

'Try?' said Franklin.

'I will,' said Ewan.

'If you can, son, if you can,' said Franklin as he stood up. 'Come back and see me either way.'

'I will,' said Ewan.

7

Andrew was alone in the Witness House. He stared out at the sun-baked street, a cul-de-sac of ten houses. Beyond bored, he was catatonic. There was no movement, not even a bird. It was never like this at home, the air was never so still, so hot and silent. Dead centre of the front lawn was a square shrub. It was so deeply hybrided, fertiliser-saturated and genetically pre-trimmed that it was a non-plant. No botanist could have discerned its species. The shrub was chosen specifically for its anonymity. The whole house was. Not only did people on the street not know the purpose of the house, they barely even perceived it as being there, as if it was built in a blind spot. Some thought there were only nine houses on the street.

The Witness House was unsettled. No one ever stayed long. Each cup in the kitchen had been used and abandoned so often it had taken on a hard, mean look. There were stacks of unloved books. Andrew flicked through one but soon tossed it back. He decided to go up to the room he shared with Ewan. That would kill about fifteen seconds. Their room was up the stairs and then a further ascent, up a ladder into the converted attic. There was a skylight in the roof. Sunlight was burning a rectangle into the carpet.

Time is too slow.

Andrew lay on the carpet and willed a coma to overcome him.

He heard the front door open and close. Footsteps came up the stairs and stopped. Andrew waited but they went no further. Not up the ladder, not into a bedroom. Andrew rolled over and dipped his head down through the opening. Ewan was loitering by his mother's door.

'Oh, hello,' said Ewan.

Andrew could tell he was interrupting something but did not care. 'Where've you been?' he asked.

'I wanted to visit my father,' said Ewan.

'Thought so,' said Andrew. 'Your ma wasn't happy about it.'

Ewan glanced at her door.

'Jones and Stirling brought her to court,' Andrew went on. 'They had guns under their jackets. Jones showed me hers. Bet you're sorry you missed that.'

Andrew grinned. Ewan sniffed, as if to say: *actually, I am not interested.* His eyes flicked towards his mother's door again.

'Why do you want to go in your ma's room?' Andrew asked.

It was easy to get the truth out of Ewan. Just ask a direct question. This was something Andrew liked about him.

'I am going to take her wedding ring,' said Ewan.

'Why?'

'To give my father. He wants it. For a good luck charm or something.'

'Cop on,' said Andrew, 'he's probably going to sell it.'

'So what if he does?' Ewan said angrily. 'He paid for it! And she won't even notice it's gone.'

Ewan seized the doorknob and went in. Andrew slid down the ladder and stood behind him. Ewan had never stolen anything in his life, it was Andrew who had the track record for theft. Andrew forgave Ewan for leaving him alone in the Witness House. The boy was clearly in a bad way. Ewan had stopped only two steps in. Sun on the window had heated the room like an oven. Dust was baking in the thick carpet. Articles of clothing lay over the duvet.

'You're thinking I won't have the guts,' Ewan said over his shoulder, 'aren't you?'

'I'm not wondering what you're going to do,' said Andrew. 'I'm wondering what *I'm* going to do.'

The heat boiled Ewan's brain. He turned, pushed out past Andrew and sat down heavily on the stairs. He only dully registered the sounds of Andrew in his mother's room. He was opening the wardrobe. Then the drawers beneath.

Andrew went down the stairs until he was eye to eye with Ewan. 'Is this it?' he asked. He held out a small box, open on its hinge. A gold band was nestled inside.

'Yes.' Ewan took the box from Andrew's palm.

Was that the right thing? Andrew wondered.

8

May kicked at the weeds in the driveway of the Black Mountain School for Gifted Catholic Girls. Mona told her weeding duty was not punishment for her outburst, just a standard summer chore, but May did not want to believe it. For the umpteenth time she checked her mobile for texts from Andrew or Ewan. None. Mona was sat in the driveway, pulling out weeds at a leisurely rate.

'If I get a suntan I'll scream,' Mona said. She tugged the brim of her floppy hat until it covered the tip of her nose.

'Ye must be hot in that gear,' said May, putting her mobile away. Mona's skirt splayed out over red and black striped tights. Purple fingerless gloves matched her lipstick. She wore a velvet waistcoat. She wore chunky boots. She looked like a bad fairy.

'If you don't like my clothes, why were you peeking in my wardrobe at lunchtime?'

May knelt to pull a weed not succumbing to

toe-power. 'Didn't say I didn't like them,' she said. 'Just, it's hot today, that's all.'

'*You*,' Mona said from under her brim, 'dress like a wee country girl with potatoes in her pockets. All wide-eyes and polished shoes.'

'Shut up,' May giggled. 'Me grandma bought me these shoes.'

'You sure she bought them?' Mona inquired. 'Or they're hers from when she was a girl?'

'NO. They're new,' said May, objecting but laughing.

'I've heaps of boots,' said Mona. 'You can have a pair if you want. If it's a pair I still like you can only borrow them. But if I'm done with them they're yours for keeps.'

May's face shone in delight. 'Thanks!'

'And I've heaps of clothes. Want to dress up after dinner?'

May nodded eagerly. Mona had so many clothes she had a wardrobe all to herself. The other girls needed only three between them.

Rosy came puffing down the driveway. She was red as a tomato by the time she got to May and Mona. She put her hands on her hips and surveyed their efforts.

'I knew rightly yous would get nowhere,' she said. 'I finished vacuuming extra fast so to come and help.'

Mona held her hands up in a mock display of helplessness. 'We're delicate,' she exclaimed.

At the bottom of the driveway, May gripped the bars

of a gate and played prisoner. It was not a convincing impression as the gates were unlocked. May could see a bus stop not far down the side road, just before the motorway slip road. Across the road the steep embankment rose, a man-made ridge running towards Hardglass. May could hear the motorway traffic above. She kicked off with one foot, swung out on the gate and looked back up at the school. Could it be home?

'What do auras look like?' May called to Rosy.

Rosy thought about it while working. 'Hard to describe,' she said. 'They're like wispy bits of smoke rising off our bodies all the time.'

May got off the gate and walked closer to Rosy. 'Will ye take a look at me aura?' she asked.

Rosy stayed concentrated on the weeds. 'Sister Perpetua already asked me to do a check-up on you, so I examined it when you were sleeping,' Rosy shot a glance at May. 'Sister Perpetua's not so bad, you know.'

May toed at a weed. 'How am I then so?'

Rosy eased another weed out of the ground. She knew how to get the roots and all. 'You're a tiny bit . . . malnourished,' she said.

May kicked at the weed. 'Not a great cook, me dad,' she said.

'When Sister Primrose goes to pick up Elizabeth's medicine she'll get you supplements as well,' said Rosy. 'They'll help build you up.'

'From now on at dinner time,' Mona added in a consoling voice, 'you can have all my turnip.'

May looked at her slender wrists. She was the smallest girl at Black Mountain, apart from Rafferty and Lizzy, of course. May had always thought growing tall was something that would start happening soon. But she was fourteen already. When would her growth spurt start? Then a wariness tiptoed across her consciousness. In a storm of black wings a dozen ravens burst from the trees and flew away. A drumming began between May's ears. It was pulsing, malignant and moving fast. Mona was talking but May did not catch the words. A wind was picking up, a wind only May felt. 'Something is coming,' she said.

Rosy knelt back on her haunches and looked around. 'What?' she asked.

May was already out of the gates and pounding up the embankment. She wanted to see the source of the beat. To Rosy and Mona her behaviour was completely inexplicable. They looked at each other.

'I suppose we should go after her,' said Mona.

At the top of the embankment the motorway suddenly opened up beneath May, four screaming lanes. May flung herself down and gripped the grass, afraid the slipstream could suck her down among the wheels. The beat was stronger now, a furious drumming on the sensitive skin of her mind. She looked to the approaching vehicles. There, galloping among cars, was a scaly red monster. Glowing eyes, horns and trailing smoke.

May realised it was not a monster. It was an articulated truck, exhausts jutting up like horns, sunlight striking off headlamps and its engine making an impatient roar identifiable above other traffic. It ran on eighteen wheels. Chained the entire length of its trailer was a red shipping container. It was big, like a steel house without windows, and there were things inside. Living things, pulsing with rage.

WeAre . . . WeAre . . . WeAre . . . WeAre . . . WeAre . . . WeAre . . .

The beat hammered down on May. She fought to get away, throwing herself back down the embankment. She hit the grass and rolled, her brain bouncing around in her skull. On her eyelids May felt a speeding rhythm of grass— sky— grass— sky— grass—

Mona and Rosy caught her halfway down. May's teeth were gritted, arms wrapped around her head. They sat her up and brushed grass off her.

'You okay?' asked Mona.

'There were creatures in the back of a truck headed for the city,' said May.

'Animals?' inquired Rosy.

'Monsters,' said May.

9

Ewan crossed the white-tiled room. He walked slowly to gain time. He wanted to identify the thick neck and bald head at his father's table. The visitor was arranging papers on the table for Franklin's inspection. The strap of his eyepatch gave it away. Ewan faltered. He wanted to complete his mission but he did not want to meet Magee.

'Well, well. Back already!' called Franklin. His words echoed between tiles. Inmates and visitors broke from their huddles, seeking the source of the full voice. Pride was a rare commodity here.

'Come on over,' continued Franklin. 'Magee, you'll remember my son. Shake his hand.'

Ewan was embarrassed. He felt accepted into a secret society and, because of his father, he already had status. He sat down. The papers before his father were covered in handwritten columns, upside down from Ewan's position. He saw the word 'Bounder' and big numbers, all in tens of thousands. Then Magee whipped the pages together in a pile. Ewan looked up and saw his father watching him.

'Don't worry about those things,' said Franklin.

'You and my lad used to pal around together when you were wee,' Magee said to Ewan. 'Remember that?'

'I do,' said Ewan.

'Won't mind if you and Dan got to be pals again,' Magee said. His eyepatch was damp, he dabbed at it with a piece of kitchen roll. 'He's fallen in with a rough crowd since, he's always gallivanting or hanging around the bus shelters. You'd be a good influence on him.'

Ewan placed the wedding ring's small box on the tabletop. He fenced it with his hands. Magee cast his one eye at it. Franklin looked at it too but knew better than to make any sudden grabs. He talked about something else.

'Don't mind Magee's patch,' he said. 'Magee's got an eye in there just like the rest of us. It's just he's got a leaky tear duct, isn't that right?'

Ewan saw a grimace of humiliation cross Magee's face. Ewan was embarrassed again, for Magee this time.

'I can't control it,' he admitted to Ewan. 'It looks as if I'm crying so I cover it up.'

'Can doctors not help, Mr Magee?'

'The doctors are useless,' Magee sighed. 'I think the problem is a reaction to handling . . . certain kinds of hardware. Still, we'll soon be rid of them.'

'We're shutting down the business for good,' said Franklin.

'I don't think dealing weapons should be called a "business",' said Ewan, in a righteous tone.

Magee half-agreed. 'A nasty business,' he said grimly.

'But still a business,' Franklin said to Ewan. 'You're the one always glued to nature programmes on telly. Life is competition. Defend what you have or it'll be taken off you. True, I imported raw materials to make weapons. Then I sold them. But weapons do not make a war, people do. People will fight with teeth and nails if they have to.'

'It's a jungle out there,' Magee contributed.

'Yeah,' said Franklin. 'Think even of trees themselves. Why do trees grow the way they do? Straight up tall with branches reaching out?'

Ewan was surprised to be suddenly talking about trees. In this tiled bunker trees were distant things. It was hard to believe they even existed. 'I don't know,' he said.

'Competition!' said Franklin. 'Have you heard this: "I think that I will never see a thing as pretty as a tree"? It's a famous poem.'

Magee interjected, 'It's more like, "I think that I shall never see, a poem lovely as a tree, a tree that looks at God all day, and lifts her leafy arms to pray . . ."'

'That's the one,' said Franklin, 'but it's complete nonsense. Trees are tall and reach for the sky because

56

they're in competition for sunlight. They need light to live. A tree has big spreading branches to keep its opponents in shadow. What's pretty about that? Make no mistake, a tree is at war with everything that might steal its light.'

'Your dad's right,' said Magee. 'But don't worry, the weapons will be gone soon. I'm collecting more tonight.'

'Pass the ring to Magee,' Franklin said suddenly to Ewan. 'Best not give it to me now. Magee'll look after it. Right?'

'Right,' said Magee. He placed his hands over the box. It was gone now. Ewan was sure he could have slipped the ring to his father without the guard noticing. Andrew was probably right. It looked like Magee was going to sell it for Franklin.

I don't care, Ewan told himself.

'Good man, Ewan,' said Franklin, relaxing now. 'You did a fine job. Right now, me and Magee have some logistics to discuss. Would you mind leaving us to it?'

Ewan nodded stiffly and stood. It was a man's meeting. Just like all those between Franklin and Magee at the kitchen table years previously, while he and Dan were in his bedroom on the PlayStation.

Outside the detention centre the street noise seemed louder than before. Ewan felt strangely threatened by the traffic and pedestrians. Any of these people could be terrorists or hit-and-run drivers. Such thoughts had never occurred to Ewan before.

10

'You said you'd take care of him,' was the first thing Ewan's mother said to Andrew when she returned with Jones and Stirling.

'He came back but sneaked off again,' said Andrew with a shrug. 'I can't watch him every second.'

'You promised,' she said.

Andrew turned to go but she grabbed his arm. Andrew's anger flashed. Part of him must have thought he was back in the schoolyard, and his hand became a fist before he recovered his cool. He pulled free and continued up to the attic room. Halfway up the stairs he turned and looked down on her.

'I'll keep my promise,' he said.

In the attic room Andrew got up on his bedside locker, opened the skylight and looked out across the rooftops. After a while he heard Ewan coming in the front door. There were sharp tones between him and his mother and attempts at negotiation from Stirling. Then the thumping of Ewan's feet on the way up.

'It's just houses for miles,' Andrew said, still gazing out the skylight.

Ewan was pacing back and forth. 'Want to go for a walk?' he asked.

'To where?' asked Andrew.

'My aunt's house.'

Ewan wanted to slip out unnoticed. They thought they had succeeded until, two streets away, they realised Jones was driving slowly alongside them. 'Get aboard,' she called. 'I'll give you a lift wherever you're headed.'

'We're fine walking, Officer Jones,' said Ewan, 'thank you.'

'Ewan,' she said. 'In.'

Andrew sat in the back with both arms stretched over the top of the seat. The back seat suited Andrew fine these days. Ewan sat in the front and directed Jones to his aunt's house.

'Your mam was very brave in court today,' Jones informed Ewan.

Silence.

'It's going to get hard for her,' Jones continued. 'Do you know what they're going to argue? That your mam is having an affair and that's why she's trying to get your father put away. Ridiculous, hmm? It goes to show how desperate they are.'

'Perhaps it's true,' said Ewan. But he saw himself in the wing mirror and looked away.

Jones sighed and pressed on. 'Your father has a whole team of solicitors. How do you suppose he affords them?'

Ewan considered this, then looked back at Andrew. 'See?' he said. 'My father has plenty of money. He doesn't need to sell . . . anything.'

Andrew just shrugged. Maybe Franklin was not going to sell the ring. He was still bad news.

'Ewan!' Jones was annoyed. 'I'm talking to you.'

Ewan faced forwards again. 'Go left here,' he said.

'You need to think about what's right,' Jones said.

'Stop,' Ewan said.

The hedge around Aunt Sybil's front garden was clipped so severely Andrew mistook it for a wall. Jones elected to wait in the car. The boys went to the front door. When Ewan pressed the buzzer, distant gongs struck, as if this was Buckingham Palace rather than a semi-detached in Hardglass.

Aunt Sybil had the face of a woman constantly seeking opportunities to be offended. It did not change much when she recognised her brother's son. She brought them into the hallway but no further. Andrew did not mind. The carpet was vacuumed so viciously its pile stood on end. Andrew felt awkward indenting it with his big blunt feet. It was a house full of furniture too clean to sit on and ugly ornaments that existed only to be polished. The air smelled like Aunt Sybil pumped a whole tin of air-freshener into it every day. It was supposed to be pleasant but really the house was just a rose-scented gas chamber. It was the kind of house the vicar would call to, drink tea and make polite conversation, all the while silently scream-ing for something, anything, to happen. Any dangerous dirty thing.

Ewan asked about his father's dog.

'Oh yes,' said Aunt Sybil, 'you can have it. I keep it in the garage. I am glad you've come because Harold and I are going away for two weeks. Up to the cara-van in Portrush.'

Getting out of town while the trial is on, thought Andrew.

'Have you visited my father?' asked Ewan.

Aunt Sybil pulled her cardigan around herself. 'I can't be seen near places like that,' she said. 'But make no mistake. I am behind him all the way. They're releasing people every day of the week with this Peace Process. Why don't they just let him go too?'

Then Aunt Sybil decided she might have said too much. She turned suspicious eyes on the strange boy, Andrew, standing on her carpet. You still had to be careful what you said in front of strangers. Whose side was this boy on? She folded her arms. 'Go on, get the dog,' she said. 'Then you'll have to excuse me. *Gardener's World* is about to begin.'

Blondie was the colour of gold. She was a golden retriever. She stood wagging her tail. Ewan attached the leash to her collar and said goodbye to Aunt Sybil. Andrew encouraged Blondie into the back seat of Jones's car with him. She laid her chin on his knee. 'Good girl, good girl,' said Andrew as he stroked her.

At the top of the road Jones took a new route.

'This is the wrong way,' said Ewan.

'We're not going straight back to the Witness House from *her* house,' said Jones.

Ewan settled in his seat patiently. 'Okay,' he said, humouring her, 'but I hardly think Aunt Sybil is involved with the criminal element.'

That was the last straw. Jones braked harshly in the middle of the street. Ewan was thrown forwards and Blondie yelped. Jones applied the handbrake with a crunch.

'A joke, is it?' she said, facing Ewan. 'But nobody's laughing. Imagine a bit of explosive this big.' Jones held her thumb and forefinger a hair's breadth apart. 'Not much but enough to blow a leg off. So, what's that? A man without a leg. But no, it's more. It's a man who can't work. It's his son's nervous disorders. It's his daughter's bitterness. It isn't just an injury. It's a tragedy that cuts into dozens of people. It *lives*. It spreads out and hooks up with other tragedies until the whole country is covered in a poisonous net. Do you understand?'

'That's history now,' Ewan protested. 'He's helping fix it.'

Jones shook her head. 'The most helpful thing Franklin can do now is go to prison. And you need to be supporting your mam. She is brave. And *important*.'

Ewan went quiet.

'Good girl,' said Andrew.

Both Jones and Ewan whipped around and looked at Andrew in the back seat. They had forgotten he was there.

Andrew stopped stroking the dog and looked back at them. 'I was talking to Blondie,' he said.

Back at the Witness House, Ewan disappeared upstairs. Andrew took Blondie for a walk. When he returned he found Stirling in the living room. He was watching the news and filling his pipe. Andrew had thought only old men smoked pipes but Stirling was younger than his da.

'I'm on night watch,' said Stirling.

Andrew managed to scoop Blondie into his arms and carry her up the ladder to the attic room. Ewan was pacing. Andrew lay on his bed and waited. He knew Ewan would make an announcement soon. It would be about what Jones said in the car.

Both their mobile phones chimed at the same time. That meant May. Ewan ignored his phone but Andrew looked at his.

'R there monsters in city?'

Andrew smiled at the cryptic message. 'Hope not.

Ewan wild enough for me', he replied.

'I've been thinking about what Jones said in the car,' said Ewan.

'Really?' said Andrew.

'I want to go to the docks tomorrow and see the weapons. My father said he rented a warehouse for them. They'll be in crates, I suppose.' Ewan sat down on the edge of his bed. 'I have to be sure he's really getting rid of them.'

'Makes sense,' said Andrew. 'Can I come with you for a change?'

11

May was sitting on the edge of her bed.

'Close your eyes,' said Mona.

May felt soft padding on her brow.

'I've put on shadow,' explained Mona. 'Don't rub it or the glitter will come off.'

May wound her fingers together. It was a struggle staying still. Before moving on to make-up Mona had plaited her hair. Two braids hung over May's shoulders. In her old school a girl with plaits would have been laughed into the ground. But now plaits were so brilliant May felt an excitement verging on nausea. Mona had given her clothes but best of all were the boots. May's toes curled with pleasure inside them. They had a cheap plasticky feel but dozens of eyelets and scarlet laces long enough to tether a boat.

'Eye pencil.' Mona named each application as she leaned in.

Mona never looked anyone in the eye but now May

fancied she could feel Mona's gaze on her eyelids. With May's eyes safely closed Mona would be, for once, looking someone square in the face.

'Tracing the lash line with liquid stuff,' announced Mona.

May felt the shimmering weight of new layers.

'Last, a stroke of highlighter under each brow . . . there. Done.'

May flicked her eyes open fast but Mona had already turned away.

May went to the mirror and looked at her changed self. It was like she had a blue butterfly wing resting over each eye. The boot's thick rubber soles made her taller. It was like looking at someone else. She liked it.

Sally walked to the dormitory. She did a triple take at May's new look. While Sally gawked May shuffled in her boots, liking attention and not liking it at the same time.

'Sister Perpetua wants to see you,' said Sally when recovered.

May went, '*Tuh.*'

Sister Perpetua was waiting outside the door. She made no comment on May's change. It was as if the view from behind her spectacles passed straight through those thin layers.

'Your training begins,' she said.

It was late. The Milky Way was a dense splatter

across the black arc of the sky. A warm breeze passed through the trees, distributing their leafy scent. The ravens slept in the upper branches. Beneath Sister Perpetua's chamber window was the stable.

'Ever ridden?' asked Sister Perpetua.

'No. I don't like horses,' said May.

'You should try it,' said Sister Perpetua. 'The sense of unity is sublime.'

Inside the stable was an inky pool of darkness. From the depth came a short blast of noise, a lippy sputter. Saint's body took form as he stepped into the starlight. He stood high yet obedient above their heads. He was jet black, as if a sheet had been cut out of the night sky and wrapped around bone and muscle, with two stars for eyes. Saint was beautiful. He knew it. And May knew he knew it. But it did not matter because he was right. Everybody knew that.

Sister Perpetua stroked his nose. 'Let's leave him and go up the field,' she said.

It took a while to climb the rough incline. May lagged behind, watching her new boots walking. Sister Perpetua stopped at the boundary wall of the school. The walls on Black Mountain were built of rough rocks, some the size of small boulders, stacked with canny skill a hundred years before. The walls stretched up the mountainside until the land grew too steep. Then, as if by exhaustion, they shrank and disappeared. In the dark, the mountain ridge could not be seen directly but you knew it was the line where complete blackness ended and stars began.

Sister Perpetua touched the stone wall. It seemed to please her. May looked towards the sky-glow above Hardglass. Saint had stayed by his stable.

'So,' said Sister Perpetua, 'open your Gift and look inside. Use it to call Saint to us.'

May emitted a sigh of profound inconvenience but opened her mind to Saint. The horse's world flowed between her ears. He was engaged with every fibre of himself. He loved the sensation of his lungs expanding, pressing against his chest as his wide nostrils vacuumed up scented air.

My lady, would you leave me here? I wait for our time. My lady . . .

Her grandma called May's Talent a window. Through it she could see into animal life. Could that mean, if she practised, animals could look back out at her? Maybe. Maybe not.

Come here to me, she thought, forcefully.

Come here to me.

Come here to me.

What would it be like to communicate with animals? It would not be a normal conversation. They would feel her instincts.

Come here to me.

Come here to me.

She opened her eyes and took a breath. Saint had not budged.

'It's not something ye get by trying hard,' said May.

'That may well be true,' said Sister Perpetua, 'but how else can one begin a spiritual task? You must try hard. When you're exhausted you must try harder. You must try and try until the trying falls away. Then you and the task will have become one.'

Come here to me.

Come here to me.

May's fingers curled into fists.

Come here to me.

Come here to me.

'Remember your breathing,' said Sister Perpetua. 'Breath him in and you out.'

Come here to me.

Come here to me, ye stupid horse.

May opened her eyes and huffed. 'It's not working for me,' she said. 'I'm getting him loud and clear. He's just not getting me. I can't control him. This Talent only goes in one direction.'

Suddenly Sister Perpetua spoke harshly. 'Me! I! Time you realise that the Gifts have little to do with you. You're trying to tap into a mystery, a mystery only God knows. And what's this talk of "control"? You're not trying to control Saint. You're trying to join him. Lose yourself to creation.'

'I don't even care!' May shouted. 'Ye try it!'

May stormed back down the field to the school. Sister Perpetua let her go. She placed her hand on the wall and contemplated it.

May threw herself into an armchair in the common room. It was almost springless, sitting in it caused its shapeless arms to inflate. The common room was across the hall from the dormitory. Its carpet was curled and its wallpaper wrinkled. There was a book-shelf overloaded with charity-shop encyclopaedias and bibles. There was a television but the girls were only allowed to watch a programme if it was boring. Rafferty was reading a book. Mona was listening to her MP3 player. Tara was delicately spooning Elizabeth's nightly medicine into her mouth. Sister Primrose twirled away from the window and smiled at May. 'I see Mona gave you a makeover,' she said. 'That was nice of her, wasn't it?'

'Are ye able to do things like us?' May asked.

'You girls are my Gifts,' Sister Primrose said sweetly. 'I'm thankful for you every day.'

May rolled her eyes. 'No, I'm talking about a special Talent, like what we have.'

You could almost see Sister Primrose shrink. 'No, not like yours,' she said, hurt.

'And what about Perpetua?'

Rafferty looked at May over the top of her book. '*Sister* Perpetua,' she said.

'Aye,' said May, 'her.'

'I don't know if Sister Perpetua has a Gift or not,' said Sister Primrose. 'She doesn't tell me everything, you know.' She hovered, unsure, before retreating from the room.

'Don't know how ye stand it here!' announced May.

Mona heard her over her music. 'It builds character,' she said before zoning out again.

'Let Elizabeth keep you company for a while,' said Tara. She pushed Elizabeth's wheelchair alongside May and left her parked there. Elizabeth was smiling, her eyes full of distance.

May fumed. This place was like a cult. It had sucked the life out of the girls. The nuns made May want to scream. Their buttoned-up collars. Their serene, glazed expressions. Their we-know-what's-good-for-ye attitude. May took care of herself, thanks very much. Still, Primrose had got her those supplements. That *was* kind, May had to admit. Mona had given her clothes and boots. May was sure Mona was going to be her friend. Rosy too. Tara might take a bit longer. May was nervous of her, she always seemed close to rage, but suddenly May's heart opened. Of course Tara was troubled. It was not easy having the Talents. May understood that. But now they had all found each other. They were a family. May could hear Sister Primrose singing in the kitchen, a dreamy traditional air. It was wonderful. May decided to go apologise to her. She would be forgiven and everything would be fine. Everything was wonderful—

'HEY,' demanded May. She leaped from the armchair. 'What's she doing to me?'

Tara slapped her knees and laughed. 'Elizabeth gets to your head, doesn't she?' she said. 'What did we tell you? She's pure love.'

Mona grinned. She could see what was going on.

May bolted for the corner and watched Elizabeth suspiciously.

Rafferty put down her book. 'Elizabeth carries positive energy around with her like a smell,' she said. 'Too bad we can't bottle it.'

'I can't believe ye *like* that,' said May. Elizabeth had reached into May's mind and massaged it, without permission. Sure, it was nice in a way but May felt violated. She stayed in the corner.

'You're all mad,' she said.

12

Andrew could remember a film where people were shrunk and had to survive in an oversized world. The docks were like that. Everything was built to a bigger scale. The roads were wider, the walls taller, the machines too massive to be allowed into the normal-sized city. The security huts were unmanned when Andrew and Ewan passed through the dock gates. Everything was silent; only an occasional truck rumbled by, throwing up dry dust clouds. There were no ships at all. The boys walked up and down long desolate piers, quietly heating up under the sun. They had been searching for hours, without results, when a truck emerged from between coal dumps. It went past, towing an empty trailer and churning up dust. Andrew covered his nose and mouth. The biggest dust particles tinkled against the ground. The driver did not see the boys. Maybe they were too small to be seen in this world.

Confident of his direction for the first time, Ewan

went the way the truck had come from. 'The man who was driving, his name is Magee,' he explained to Andrew. 'He works for my father.'

Tonnes of coal were heaped both sides of the road. It was a valley of black hills. Further on, they passed between two grey hills of gravel. Then two white hills of salt. It seemed chunks of the earth were being scooped out of one place, shipped across oceans and used to build hills somewhere else. Was this how the world turned?

Beyond the valleys was wharf thirteen, long enough for an aeroplane to land had cranes not been in the way. Warehouses overlooked the wharf, doors open and all empty. Andrew and Ewan walked to the quay-side. The water was dead calm and slick with oil, the surface ran with a pattern of chemical rainbows. Half way along the wharf an old freighter was docked. It was called the *Bounder* and was Nigerian registered. It seemed every part of the *Bounder* was dented, rusted, cracked or crooked. Stretched out under the sun, the metal deck would have been too hot to touch. The ship was high in the water, obviously empty. There were no crew to be seen. Opposite the freighter was the only locked warehouse on wharf thirteen. One of its corrugated panels was bent. Using both hands Andrew widened the gap. Ewan slipped in and Andrew followed.

Before noticing the smell, the cool dark interior of

74

the warehouse came as a relief. The warehouse was huge but felt flimsy, a thin-skinned cathedral. The roof supports, like 'A's stretched wide, were lost in shadow. Here and there in the roof were holes left by bolts that had fallen out. Sunlight beamed through the holes like lasers, piercing the dark and making bright patches on the ground no bigger than coins.

Twelve red shipping containers were stacked high. They were bunched together in three stacks, each four containers tall, creating a kind of apartment block. Some had numbers painted on. The containers were moulded with ridges and slots so as to fit together but some were too bashed-about for the system to work. It was sheer weight that held the containers on top of each other. They were stacked to the roof and stank to high heaven.

The boys were held back by the stench. It was the clang of meaty decay. It leaked from the containers and came from the tarry black soup oozing from under their doors. The ooze was like death, liquidised and squeezed out.

'These have to be the weapons,' said Ewan. 'Looks like they're going to be taken away by the ship out there. My father was telling the truth.'

'What's the stink?'

'Perhaps it's used to cover up the smell of explosives.'

'Some containers are wrapped in chains,' Andrew pointed out, 'weird.'

The tar was pooled under the containers' ends, where the latched doors were, but along the side they could approach the containers and touch the lowest. '29' was painted on it.

'Up there!' said Andrew suddenly. He was pointing up at a movement among the roof supports, a swift ripple in the shadows. Silently, it landed on top of the containers and was gone.

'I think it was a boy,' said Ewan, straining his neck.

'I bet he moved because he was afraid of being seen,' said Andrew. 'But it backfired. Him moving was the reason I saw him.'

'Come down!' Ewan shouted. 'These containers are not your property.'

No reply. Nothing.

'Fancy going up after him?' asked Andrew.

'No thank you,' said Ewan.

The boy saved them the effort, and in acrobatic style. He swung off the topmost container, one hand staying gripped to the corner and his legs swished out in an arc. The boy's knees hit the side of the container and for a split second he dangled. Even on his outstretched arm the container was taller than him. His feet had nowhere to go, so he just dropped. Andrew and Ewan gasped and stepped back. The boy dropped to the next container top and stopped. He had clamped on with both hands. A momentary pause and he dropped again. Clinging to the top of the base container he was now a safe distance from the ground. He jumped away, turned in the air and landed neatly in front of Andrew and Ewan. He wore sneakers without socks or laces, sun-bleached shorts, a too-big shirt and a questioning expression. 'What do you know of these boxes?' he asked.

'We know you shouldn't be swinging around on them,' said Ewan.

'What do you know of what is *inside* them?'

Ewan was about to answer but decided to take control. He was bigger. He had a big friend. He asked the questions around here.

'What do *you* know of what's inside?' he said.

'I know it is evil,' said the boy. 'That is enough.'

'They smell evil,' said Andrew, trying to find something they could all agree on. 'So, who are you?'

'I am Akeem,' said the boy.

'And where do you come from, Akeem?'

'Lagos,' he said.

Andrew looked to Ewan. Akeem could tell Andrew had never even heard of his city. It was one of the biggest cities in the world.

'Ha!' said the boy vengefully. 'I have never heard of Hardglass!'

'Then why are you here?' said Ewan.

'Everybody has to be somewhere,' the boy said.

'Perhaps nobody told you but there was fighting here for years,' said Ewan, 'but now it's over. We're having a Peace Process. There're weapons in these containers. More will be arriving over the next few days. Then they're going to be got rid of.'

Akeem made a derisive hoot. 'You might call it getting "rid of" but for me it is different,' he said. 'They will be loaded on the boat outside and exported to my homeland. How is selling weapons part of making peace?'

'They're not being sold,' objected Ewan, 'they're being got rid—'

'They are being sold!' cut in the boy with an emphatic nod. 'I hear it from the roof. Just now the fat man was here, the man with the . . .' He put a hand over one eye.

'Eyepatch,' offered Andrew.

'The man with the eyepatch,' Akeem continued. 'He talks into his mobile phone. He names names that are feared in my homeland, the warlords of the provinces. He will sell them the dogs for ten thousand pounds each.'

'Dogs?' said Andrew.

'That is what he calls them,' said Akeem. 'I do not know what they are but they live and they are evil.'

Until now Ewan was happy that Hardglass would to be free of the weapons. His father was making amends. But now things were more complicated. Were the weapons being exported for profit? Would they be used to kill people somewhere else? And—

'What do you mean "they live"?' demanded Ewan.

Akeem took on the exaggerated expression of someone telling a ghost story. 'Sometimes I hear things moving inside the boxes,' he said.

Andrew and Ewan looked again at the containers towering over them.

'I will stop these boxes going to my homeland,' said Akeem. 'You bred these beasts. You can keep them.'

'But how will you stop them?' said Andrew.

Akeem pointed down the warehouse to where a forklift truck was parked. 'The eyepatch man uses that to take the boxes off his truck and stack them. I have watched him from the roof. I think I can drive it.'

The forklift was similar to those in Andrew's hometown but, like every machine in the docks, it was super-sized. It was as squat and wide as two cars. Its tyres bulged.

'When all the boxes are here I will take them outside,' said Akeem. 'One by one I will drop them in the sea.'

Ewan turned on him. 'You will not!' he shouted.

It was the first time Andrew had ever heard Ewan shout in anger.

'It is God's will,' said Akeem defiantly.

Then Ewan did something more shocking than shouting. He hit the boy. It was a weak first-timer's punch but Akeem was light. He fell. His head struck the container hard enough to make a dull *dong*.

Horrified, Andrew locked his arms around Ewan. It was hard to tell by Ewan's face if he would keep attacking the boy. An angry expression is very like a frightened one.

Akeem was rubbing the back of his head. 'Woooeee,' he said.

'We're sorry,' said Andrew. 'Are you hurt?'

But Akeem ignored him. He had heard something else. He shifted position until one ear was against the container. 'Did you hear?' he asked.

'What?' asked Andrew.

This time Akeem did not hit the container. The container hit him.

The steel side was punched out by an internal explosion. In a millisecond it went from flat to puffed out. Stretched metal bowled Akeem forwards. Flipped clean over, he hit Andrew and Ewan and they all landed in a heap. The higher containers wavered in reaction to the jolt. They wobbled outwards. The boys below held their breaths. The next two seconds lasted a long time. With a steely squeal and resounding clash the containers banged back into vertical. The boys breathed again.

But there were new noises. The violence of container twenty-nine set off others. The containers above and beside began to shift and clank. Soon all twelve containers were ringing and knocking, driven by whatever was inside. The next big jolt came from a container directly on top of twenty-nine, it was one of the containers wrapped in chains. It jumped and expanded. The chains smithereened, every link exploding in the same instant. Hot iron screamed like a spray of bullets. Pieces punctured the walls. Some even shot to the back and struck off that distant wall. The top container jumped and landed again with a mighty *CLANG* but the slots and ridges no longer accepted each other. Loose, the top container turned in the slow laziness of a thing with enormous weight. Metal ground against metal. The tower swayed. Nothing was going to stop these containers taking a tumble.

The boys knew there was no outrunning it. The smash-zone would be thirty metres long.

The heavy grind of friction became a groan of relief. For a moment the top container hung in the air, unsupported, impossible. Akeem and Ewan ran and dived out the side. Andrew was still looking straight up at the container. A thought flashed across his mind. The thought was this: during wars, during air raids, people might sometimes have glimpsed a bomb as it fell to ground. If it was daylight, if they were outside and happened to glance up, they saw the bomb that was about to kill them. Maybe, in that fraction of a second, they had time to understand what they were seeing. Maybe they saw details, like the serial number printed on the side. Maybe they had time to feel afraid. Then, what they were seeing, along with everything they ever saw, and everything they ever felt, was smeared across the burning earth.

The container rushed to ground. Andrew ran and leaped. 'COVER YOUR EARS,' he was screaming.

The container's collision with the ground made more than a noise, it was a blasted sound wave, too loud to be heard. Displaced air lifted the boys and tossed them away. For a split second the ground behaved as water, a ripple ran through it. It radiated out and shook the walls of the warehouse. Another container fell and hit with a hundred-tonne punch. Steel compressed and expanded. Black tar splattered wide. The top container of the middle stack then slid loose and crashed on top of the others. It bent into an angle and sat still. No more fell. The containers settled into aftermath. The clanging from inside them stopped. After the sustained banging, grinding, screeching and crashing it was the silence that was deafening.

Somebody said, 'Run.'

The container doors had all held. The things inside fought no more, disturbed at the hurt and fright they had caused themselves. The boys were long gone when a low moan emerged from a fallen container. It was joined from inside other containers. Muffled howls added to the strange choir. Each flat lonely note combined into one long hymn of misery. It swelled, reached a crescendo, then faded away.

13

That morning May had an idea. She went into the trees around the school. The sunlight was green passing through the leaves. Just when she seemed to be arriving at the thickest part, the branches opened. A space had been cleared by the death of an oak. It was struck by lightning years before. The trunk was carbonised but still standing, all but its thickest limbs had fallen off. Surrounded by healthy trees, each dripping with fifty thousand leaves, the blasted oak was stark but darkly dignified. It was the favourite perch of the ravens. May looked up at the raven perched on it now. Its black wing matched the black branch. Maybe this was the kind of leaf that grew from a burnt tree. Not green but black. Not smooth and veined but feathered and beaked.

From the raven May felt the clear consciousness of high air, it was like an invigorating gust.

TheLandTurns BeneathMe ItSeeksMyApproval
TheLandTurns BeneathMe

May thought ravens were far better than horses.

Next to the raven one spindly twig had survived the blast. A single burnt acorn hung from it, the only acorn on the entire tree. May decided this would be her prize. She concentrated on the acorn, she concentrated on the raven, she concentrated on both together.

'Bring me the acorn. Bring me the acorn,' she recited out loud before letting her voice slip under.

Bring me the acorn.

Bring me the acorn.

No reaction from the bird. May broke concentration and caught her breath. Classes would be starting soon. May wanted the raven to take the acorn in its beak and deliver it to her. Then she could show the acorn to everyone. She concentrated again.

Bring me the acorn.

Bring me the acorn.

But the raven ignored her. It did not know nor care what she wanted. It launched, dived onto rising currents and spiralled up and away.

During class May watched the ravens through the window. She was frustrated, desperate to try again. Luckily school days were short at Black Mountain. Sister Perpetua taught English, poems about cutting turf, falling in ditches and being miserable. Sister Primrose taught History and Irish. Rafferty taught Maths. After classes books were shoved aside. Lunch was eaten and tea drunk by the bucket load. Sally read out the chore list. May, Mona and Rosy were on weeding duty again.

May returned to the blasted oak. The same raven was cawing from its branch. This time May put her hands against the black bark. Maybe the trunk would help channel her desire to the raven.

Bring me the acorn.

Bring me the acorn.

Twenty minutes later May stomped from the trees and kicked gravel down the driveway. The raven had ignored her. Mona and Rosy were weeding by the gates. May jumped onto a gate and swung on it a while. She nearly fell off in surprise when a bus motored by. It pulled in at the stop. May looked at the bus's square back. It promised adventure. She ran for it.

'May!' shouted Rosy. 'What are you doing?'

Mona chased after May. Rosy gave in and did too.

'I've an idea,' said May at the door of the bus. 'Let's go to the city and find a Protestant with the Talents. If we find one we can bring her back and show the nuns.'

'What?' said Rosy, leaning on her thighs and panting. 'You mean like a *specimen*?'

'Relax, will ye!' said May. 'We'll be back soon.'

May jumped on the bus before realising something. 'Do ye have any money?' she asked.

'I'll pay.' Mona pulled a wallet from her back pocket. 'Let's hightail it outta here.'

When the bus was on the motorway Rosy looked over her shoulder and watched the school disappear into the folds of the mountain. 'They'll be annoyed at us,' she said.

'Nightmare,' said Mona. She slapped her palms to her cheeks like the famous painting, *The Scream*. 'You don't think they'll make us weed the driveway, do you?'

May was not used to public transport. She swung on the handrails while the old people tutted. After a while she dropped into the seat in front of Mona and Rosy. Kneeling on it, she faced back at them.

'What'll we see I wonder?' said May.

'Something I don't know if my poor heart can take,' said Mona.

'What?' May asked.

'Boys,' announced Mona. She grimaced and gripped the top of May's seat, impersonating someone with a fifty-year frustration. 'Been a mighty long while since I clapped eyes on a boy,' she said.

'That reminds me,' said May. 'I'll ring me friends.' She dropped into her seat and pulled out her mobile. The only numbers in her contact list were Andrew and Ewan. She tried one, then the other. Their mobile phones were switched off.

The motorway curved around the mountain and

Hardglass was spread before them. There was a wide band of suburbia, rows of blue slate and red brick. The centre was packed with gleaming office blocks. Motorways arched and reached cleanly from one place to another. Ferries were coming and going on the glittering sea beyond.

City centre was the last stop. May jumped off the bus and her boots bounced on the pavement. She stood poised, a huntress dropped suddenly among an abundance of game. The streets were full of people shopping. May, Mona and Rosy bobbed, weaved and skipped along. They pointed at things. They stared in shop windows. On one corner a man was roaring through a megaphone about the flames of hell. He wore a black overcoat despite the heat. Like the blasted oak he was left clear space, the shoppers giving him wide berth.

'Repent!' he bellowed. 'Time is short!'

'Don't mind him,' said Mona. She led May and Rosy to a square. May gasped. Crowds of teenagers were hanging around. They had coloured hair, wore skull jewellery, drainpipe jeans and fingerless gloves. They were falling off skateboards, free-running walls, screaming and gossiping. There were dozens and dozens of them. The boys had loud voices and firmly owned the ground they stood on. The girls walked arm in arm, forming great chains that swept all before them. It was like a riot that did not go anywhere, just stayed in the same spot pulsing in and out. To these teenagers the city was a playground. The old divisions of Hardglass were not for them. The past was rejected, the future unconsidered, they lived entirely in the swirl of the present. May was enthralled.

'Most of them are lacking in iron,' Rosy commented. 'They should eat broccoli.'

Mona dashed to a cash machine and inserted her bank card. She drummed on the machine while waiting for her balance. Then she punched the air and hissed: 'Score!' She withdrew a heap of money. 'Let's shop,' she said.

A shop nearby sold, among other things, hair dye, skull jewellery, drainpipe jeans and fingerless gloves. The air was heavy with incense. There was little room to move between clothes rails, poster racks and cases of colourful glass pipes. Mona dragged May around.

'Your bog-trotting days are over,' Mona declared, holding clothes against May's frame.

With an armful of gear Mona claimed the changing room. She pulled May in and whipped the curtain shut.

'But—' May began.

'Don't worry,' said Mona. 'I've got the money.'

May had never undressed in front of anyone but knew girls in Black Mountain did it all the time. She began immediately because she did not want time to chicken out. She hated the sight of her twiggy arms.

'You're so white,' she said to Mona.

'I know,' said Mona, surprised by the obvious observation, 'that's how I like it.'

May tried something on and looked at herself uncertainly. Mona whipped a top from its hanger and pulled it on over her head. It was tartan, with a lot more zips and buckles than strictly necessary.

'Where do ye get the money?' May asked.

Mona examined herself in the mirror. 'My parents put it in my bank account for me,' she said. 'But it's like, totally unpredictable. Sometimes I don't get a penny for months. Then I get a big lump in one go.'

'Can they not ring and say when they're giving ye some?' asked May.

'No,' said Mona. 'When we realised I'd an ability they freaked out. I was using it on people. On the teachers, on kids, especially bullies. I was a nightmare. My parents heard about Black Mountain School and enrolled me at the speed of light. I hated it. Cried for a week. At the Easter holidays I went home and guess what? They'd moved and hadn't told anyone where they'd gone.'

Mona rejected the tartan top. She pulled it off and dropped it on the floor.

'They put money in my account sometimes but we've no contact,' she said. 'Sister Perpetua says I'm better off without them. She says I shouldn't even spend their money. She says Black Mountain is my family now.'

Rosy whipped open the curtain. 'Sister Perpetua is right,' she said.

May and Mona objected loudly to being exposed to the whole shop. Rosy squeezed in the changing room with them and pulled the curtain behind her. They were all squashed together.

'We *are* your family,' continued Rosy. 'Lots of girls at Black Mountain have been treated bad. But now you've got us. We're your sisters.'

Mona looked towards her feet. 'Thanks,' she said.

Pressed tight to her new friends, May felt the urge to share. 'Me mam went off when I was a baby,' she said. 'Me dad would never accept me for what I was. The whole town laughed at me and he let them. He's useless. I don't care if I never see him again.'

She stopped and swallowed. Rosy wrapped an arm around her.

'Now I'll tell yous something,' said Rosy. 'Never tell anyone, right? It's a secret.' A cheeky grin spread across her face. 'Yous don't need to go looking for a Protestant with the Talents. You've already got one.'

'Ye?' said May.

'Black Mountain is the only school of its sort in the country,' Rosy explained. 'Mam and dad were determined to get me in. So when they met Sister Perpetua they let on to be Catholic. Some parents will do anything to get their children into the right school.'

'I always thought you'd a Protestant look about you,' said Mona.

They stood for a while, contently squashed. Mona had her face to the mirror, looking into her own eyes. 'You want to know my secret now, don't you?' she said.

It was true. Both May and Rosy burned with curiosity.

'Only if you want to tell us,' said Rosy.

'When I look in people's eyes,' Mona said slowly, 'I know when they're going to die. I feel it. I've never been wrong.'

May and Rosy's minds reeled with the implications. How would people treat you, knowing you could tell when they would die? Even if no one knew of your ability, what was it like seeing death in the eyes of everyone you met? They realised it was not an ability to envy.

'Don't dare ask me to look in your eyes,' Mona said fiercely. 'People have wanted me to. Sometimes I did it. They were always sorry.'

'We won't ask,' said Rosy solemnly.

'Never,' said May.

'But, Mona,' Rosy inquired, 'do you know when *you're* going to die?'

'I've always known,' she said. 'Since I was old enough to look in a mirror and understand. I'll be about fifty-five.'

'Fifty-five!' exclaimed May. 'That's really old.'

Rosy shook her head sadly. 'No it's not, May, not really.'

Mona was not listening to either of them. She was looking into the mirror. Into the only eyes she ever looked into.

14

Ewan rang just as May was about to get on the bus back to Black Mountain. She asked Mona and Rosy to go on without her and met the boys halfway to the docks. She hugged them both.

'You look . . . different,' said Ewan.

'Thanks,' said May.

Andrew was smiling broadly. He was glad to have them all back together. 'Do you like the big smoke?' he asked.

'I wish I was in the big smoke,' said May. 'But the school is miles out. It's just a big smelly old farm-house.'

'We've found something on the docks,' said Ewan. 'Shipping containers with living things in them. We want you to use your superpower on them.'

May laughed. 'Don't call it that!' she said. 'Wait till ye hear about the other girls in Black Mountain. They all have different Talents.'

'Tell us while we're walking,' said Ewan. He already was.

At wharf thirteen May whooped and ran to the waterside. 'Seals,' she said.

'I don't see any,' said Andrew.

'Neither do I.'

May lay so most of her torso was over the water. She dipped down, supporting herself with her palms flat against the quayside. Her plaits fell straight and her face turned red. She peered into the dark underside of the wharf, a forest of concrete pillars. 'Too dark to see them,' she said, 'but there are loads of them back there.'

She hoisted herself back up.

'I still want to teach you to swim,' said Andrew.

'And I still want ye to teach me,' said May. 'Ugh! I've dust all over me.'

Ewan was walking on ahead, passing through the shadows of the cranes.

'These things Ewan wants you to see,' Andrew said quietly, 'they belong to his da.'

'I never liked the sound of him,' said May.

They were under a crane when they heard a rapid rhythm of hands slapping girders. 'This is Akeem,' said Andrew.

Akeem shinned down a leg of the crane. He descended head first, then did a backflip and landed on his feet.

'This is May,' said Andrew.

Akeem made a bow.

'Pleased to meet you. May I call you May?'

'You may.'

'Okay.'

Ewan pointed. 'They're in that warehouse,' he said to May.

'I know,' she said.

A beat was playing on her mind. Ewan had to coax her under the bent panel and into the warehouse. It was hours since the havoc. The semi-collapsed stacks were just as they had left them. May whimpered and hung back by the entrance. The boys were repelled by the stench but to May the containers radiated an emotional stench, so strong she did not notice the physical smell.

we ... are ... we ... are ... we ... are ... we ... are ... we ... are ...

'One of those crates went by me school,' said May. 'Whatever's in them, they're calmer now. They aren't always so calm.'

'We found that out,' said Andrew.

'Woooeee,' said Akeem.

'Are they asleep?' asked Ewan.

'They're not the kind of things that sleep,' she said. 'They just ... *are.*'

Akeem looked at May wide-eyed but did not doubt her. He was always open to the possibility of sorcery.

'But what are they?' asked Ewan.

we ... are ... we ... are ... we ... are ... we ...

May backed away. The beat made her sick. 'They are what they are. Not animals. Monsters. They weren't born, they can't die, they just *are*.' She tasted bile coming up with her words. 'There's millions of them creeping about. Millions, Ewan, millions. They're like a disease.'

The boys backed away as well.

'I want to go now,' said May. She wanted to be near the seals. Being with them would wash her mind.

'But what do they want?' asked Ewan.

May shuddered. 'What do monsters ever want? They want to kill.'

'You're sure that makes them monsters?' demanded Ewan.

'A thing that kills is always a monster,' said Akeem.

May thought of Andrew. 'Only if they kill for no reason,' she said. 'It's different if they're forced to.'

Andrew did not say anything.

'Can I go now?' May pleaded.

'Let the lady go,' said Akeem, 'she is distressed.'

But Ewan pushed on. 'How can there be millions of them?' he said. 'They'd leak out. Those containers aren't airtight.'

He was right. The teeming monsters were obviously not loose in the containers. Inside, they had to be within another vessel. May fought down nausea and tried to feel into the space between the beats. Moments later she broke away. 'Dogs,' she said simply. 'One in each crate.'

The boys looked at the containers anew.

'How can dogs be alive in there?' asked Andrew. May tried to separate the dogs from the monsters. It was not easy. They were closely linked.

.. .. *gagagaggagag* ... ...
... ... *hgggghghg* ... ...
... *sassssas* ... ...
.. .. *ququququququququ* ... ...
fafaafafaafa ... ... *gagagggaga gagag* ... ... *hgghghghg* ... ...
... ... *sasasas* ... ...
.. .. *ququququququququ* ...

'I don't think the dogs are alive,' she said, 'not in the usual way. Their bodies are all stretched and twisted. The monsters are inside them, controlling them. I want to go home!'

May turned and ran. Back outside, she put distance between herself and the warehouse before sitting on the quayside. The contrast was total. Here was blue water, as opposed to black tar on the warehouse floor. Here was sea breeze, as opposed to the stench between the warehouse walls. Here were playful seals, as opposed to the monsters swarming in the bodies of undead dogs.

May realised she had called Black Mountain 'home'.

The boys emerged from the warehouse.

'You two hold off on any schemes,' Ewan was saying to Andrew and Akeem. 'I am going to visit my father.'

15

The guard hung up the internal line and shook his head. 'He's out of court but declining your visit,' he said.

'It's important,' said Ewan helplessly. His father refused to see him? It was a slap in the face.

'No one can be forced to accept a visitor,' said the guard.

Ewan resolved himself. 'I'll be back,' he said, 'in a minute.'

On the pavement Ewan took out his mobile phone and sent a text: 'See me or I go to wharf thirteen and open containers'.

Soon Ewan was scanned and admitted. Franklin was at his usual table in the white-tiled room, his top button undone and his tie loosened. His chair was sideways along the table rather than under it, legs stretched out and his head slanted to watch his son approach. There was something slovenly and cruel about Franklin's posture. Aggression lay coiled inside, disguised as indifference.

'Open a container and you'll be dead in seconds,' he said as soon as Ewan sat.

'What's in them?'

'Weapons.'

'Monsters.'

'Eh?'

'Monsters,' repeated Ewan.

That silenced Franklin. He retreated, recalculated, made another move. 'Weapons that happen to be made from living things,' he said, 'creatures called the Furies.'

'The Furies. You made them?' asked Ewan.

'No, an arms manufacturer called *Honoris Causa* did that. They didn't engineer them from scratch. The Furies have been around for thousands of years, living in the ground. *Honoris Causa* found a hive, dug them up and genetically modified them to purify their instincts. I invested in six hundred tubes of them.'

'Then you put them into dogs,' Ewan said.

Franklin could not conceal his surprise at Ewan's knowledge.

'Well, well. How'd you know that?'

'I've got talented friends.'

Franklin watched Ewan for a clue that was never given.

'Dogs have talents of their own,' said Franklin. 'Talents that combine with the Furies and together make powerful weapons. And dogs are *loyal*. You might learn something from them yourself.' Franklin leaned back in his chair. 'The dogs are history now anyway. Hardglass will soon be rid of them. You won't have to worry about them any more.'

'Nigerians will instead,' said Ewan. 'You're not really getting rid of them. You're exporting them.'

Franklin dismissed the issue with the wave of a hand. 'Who cares? They'll be out of this country.'

'They'll just be somewhere else, killing other people,' said Ewan. 'It's not the end. It's just redistributing murder. You're right: weapons do not make a war, people do. But it's wrong to take advantage of this situation for money. And that's the only reason you're doing it. Money.'

Ewan jolted as his father pounced. But Franklin was only out of his seat a split second before dropping into it again. 'You're just like *her*,' he hissed. 'Nothing I earned was ever for me. It was always for you and *her*. But I'll get out, sooner or later, and the profits from exporting the dogs will be waiting for me.'

The idea of Franklin free was suddenly terrifying to Ewan.

Franklin looked away a few seconds, gathering himself. 'I'll still spend it on you,' he continued, calm and conciliatory now. 'University, or whatever you want.'

'I don't want to live on the profits of war,' said Ewan.

Franklin regarded his son coldly. 'What do you think you've been living on all your life?' he asked.

Ewan stood. His seat fell back and bounced off the floor.

'Visit again,' said Franklin. He stood and made a smile. His teeth reflected the white tiles. 'But don't go back to the docks.'

16

It was after dark when May stepped off the bus at Black Mountain. Outside the gates of the school loomed the silhouette of a strange beast, three metres tall, two heads and a tail. It was Sister Perpetua on her horse. May had skipped chores and missed dinner. There was bound to be trouble now.

'So, have you continued training?' Sister Perpetua asked.

'Ye saw I can't do it,' said May.

'Faith, May, faith,' said Sister Perpetua.

May emitted a suffering sigh. 'I'll do extra chores to make up for what I missed today,' she said.

Sister Perpetua looked up towards the school. 'If you wish,' she said, 'but I doubt the other girls will think it necessary. We understand that joining Black Mountain School is a difficult adjustment. Rafferty ran away three times in her first year. We're an unusual family.'

May could not believe it. What did a girl have to do to get punished around here?

'Ye need to make up your mind,' said May. 'Is this place a family or a school?'

'Which do you think?' asked Sister Perpetua. Her expression was inscrutable. Stars were reflected in the round lenses of her spectacles.

'I think it's a home for outcasts and . . . freaks,' said May.

Saint spluttered and clopped back and forth. May jumped. Sister Perpetua calmed him with a hand upon his neck.

'You need to develop a higher opinion of the girls of Black Mountain,' said Sister Perpetua. 'This, in turn, will help you develop a higher opinion of yourself.'

May went quiet.

'So, would you like to train some more with Saint now?' asked Sister Perpetua. 'Or have you had a long enough day already?'

'No thanks,' May was looking at her boots, 'I want to go in now.'

'So be it,' Sister Perpetua said. 'I'm going for a canter.'

She snapped the rein. A moment later Saint's tail whooshed away into the dark.

May walked up the driveway. Sally was sitting on the front steps reading a newspaper by the hall light.

'Where's Tara?' May asked.

'Tonight was her turn to go to the supermarket with Sister Primrose,' Sally said.

Sure enough, the little car belonging to the school was gone from its place.

'Where's Elizabeth?' asked May. This was what she had wanted to know in the first place. Normally asking for Tara amounted to the same thing.

'She's in the common room.'

Elizabeth was alone and faced towards the window in her wheelchair. She crooked her head in May's direction but May was not sure Elizabeth really saw her, maybe she was just attracted to the shift in the light. May pushed one of the armchairs alongside her. Then she took a deep breath and sat in it. Side by side May and Elizabeth looked out the window.

It seemed a long time had passed when Rafferty came in. May looked over her shoulder and beamed at her.

'Heard you were back,' said Rafferty, smiling. She took a seat by the bookshelf. Sally came in. Mona came in, music blasting in her ears. They all saw May turned towards the window with Elizabeth and did not interrupt. May nestled in her armchair and her heart swelled with joy. It was wonderful just being here with all her new friends. Everything was wonderful.

Lizzy was running around upstairs. 'What's up with her?' Rafferty wondered aloud.

When Rosy came in she immediately saw the collapse in Elizabeth's aura. No longer rising like smoke, it was pouring from her weightily and creeping the carpet like fog.

'Elizabeth's sick,' she said.

May jumped to her feet. Her eyes darted about Elizabeth's body but she could see nothing wrong. Her eyes were bright as ever. Rosy knelt before Elizabeth and held her two hands.

'Her lungs have collapsed. She'll soon stop breathing,' she said. She looked at everybody and made the essential one-word statement, 'Ambulance.'

May whipped out her mobile and dialled the emergency number. She requested an ambulance but then, sliding down the cliff face of panic, she was uselessly blurting, 'Elizabeth's dying! Elizabeth's dying!'

Sally snatched the mobile out of May's hand. She took it so neatly, and May's dread was so deep, that May continued to shout into her hand.

'My name is Sally Green,' Sally reported. 'We're at Black Mountain School, take exit four from the motorway west. We're beside the exit. The patient is profoundly disabled. Both lungs have collapsed. Hurry.'

Lizzy went by in a tizzy. Her dismay was intense as any but independent and isolated. Sally seized her by the shoulders and stared at her hard. When released Lizzy left the room with purpose.

'She'll make sure the gates are open,' said Sally.

Elizabeth was smiling. Nothing hinted at the turmoil inside her. Rosy, holding Elizabeth's hands, looked at the others. 'She's fading,' she said.

There was nothing to do but suffer time's slowness. Mona leaned into the wall with resignation on her face. Rafferty sat on the stairs and prayed. May ran back and forth. *Please let her be all right. Please let her be all right.* She ran outside, willing the ambulance faster. Headlights were streaking along the motorway. They might have been satellites orbiting overhead for all the help they were. On the blasted oak the ravens awoke and shuffled their wings.

Elizabeth's eyes were greying.

'The ambulance is here!' Lizzy shouted through the window.

'Let's lift Elizabeth outside,' said Sally.

The tallest girls, Sally and Rosy, grabbed the handles of Elizabeth's wheelchair. Mona and Rafferty gripped the footrests. One, two, three and they hoisted Elizabeth into the air. They brought her out and set the wheelchair in the driveway. Elizabeth was still smiling. The approaching siren sounded like a robot crying. The ambulance swung, lights blazing, up the driveway and stopped. As if synchronised the doors popped open and two paramedics were out.

'We'll take her straight in,' one said. They put a mask over Elizabeth's mouth while a platform at the back of the ambulance was lowered for her wheel-chair. The girls were calmed by the paramedics' uniformed professionalism. May stopped running about. Rosy told the paramedics about Elizabeth's requirements. They nodded unquestioningly, like two soldiers outranked. May realised the paramedics had encountered Rosy before, or at least heard stories of her. Rosy and her ability were probably whispered about in city hospitals. Rosy was a mysterious rumour. Rosy was legend.

The ambulance ripped away, spraying gravel. The girls watched it go with their hands to their faces. Rosy wanted to do something. She decided to make tea. Lots of tea for everyone.

The ambulance was just gone when the school's little car came burning up the driveway. Tara was out before the car stopped.

'Who?' she demanded.

'Elizabeth,' said Rafferty. 'Rosy saw something wrong with her lungs.'

Tara charged to the front door. It seemed to fling itself open before her. Rosy ran to the far side of the table as Tara stormed the kitchen.

'What's wrong with Elizabeth?' she demanded.

Rosy raised her hands in placation. 'Tara, please. Try to stay calm.'

'What's WRONG with Elizabeth!' Tara was bright red.

'Her lungs collapsed but don't—'

'HER LUNGS!'

A plate skidded across the table and hit the floor.

'But don't worry,' said Rosy, backing away. 'It's happened before—'

'COLLAPSED!'

'We can go visit her tomorrow,' said Rosy, her back against the broom closet.

'VISIT?'

Above, the tube of the fluorescent light shattered. It rained pieces of curved glass, followed by a cloud of white dust descending to the tabletop.

'Tara, please.'

There was a crackling noise. The tiles under Tara's feet fractured into fine lines. The force spread. Cracks radiated across the floor.

'I don't WANT TO VISIT,' she roared.

Tiles went up in a wave, leaping straight from their grouting.

'I WANT ELIZABETH!'

Bags of flour, boxes of oats and sacks of pasta all blew their tops. Buttons flew from the radio. The glass front of the microwave cracked.

'I WANT ELIZABETH!'

Hanging pots and pans clattered together. Plates launched from cupboards and flew across the kitchen. They smashed against the walls or collided in mid-air. The chairs lurched from under the table.

'I WANT ELIZABETH!'

Rosy sank to the floor, covering her face. 'Please be calm,' she was saying, unheard. She crawled under the table for protection but the table shifted, its legs producing a bass note as they dragged across the floor. Rosy crawled to keep under it.

'IWANTELIZBETH!'

Pieces of tile were picking up, shifting and gathering. A power was drawing them together, lifting them into the air. Cutlery rose and joined the swirl. The window, divided into square panels, pumped in and out until it too exploded and added more litter to the flow. Everything began to whip around. The splintered remains of chairs were sucked up into the collection of shards, food, bits of glass and smashed delft that was now spinning furiously around the room.

'IWANTELIZBETHIWANTELIZBETH!'

The whirlwind of broken things was grinding itself to dust and getting denser by the second. It sounded like a sandblaster. It *was* a sandblaster. It tore through the plaster on the walls and exposed the brickwork. In the centre of the hurricane was Tara. Her heart pumped like a volcano, drawing energy from the earth itself. Her hair frizzed in every direction. She did not know where she was. She did not know her own name. The words 'I want Elizabeth' emerged from her neck but in a garbled and extended roar, -

110

throat-stretching and inhumanly loud. Her face was red. Her knuckles were white. Her eyes popped from her head.

Sister Perpetua and Sister Primrose stooped beneath the thickest part of the spinning ring and pushed in. Instantly they were scratched and bleeding. They burst into the eye of the storm. An inch-long shard of glass buried itself into Sister Perpetua's arm. She looked at it with distaste, pulled it out and dropped the bloody piece on the floor. Sister Primrose had her arms around Tara.

'IWANTELIZABETH!' Tara was roaring at the ceiling.

'We know, we know,' said Sister Primrose, trying to protect her from the storm. Sister Perpetua put her hands on Tara's shoulders. Next Lizzy rolled in. She hugged Tara's ankles.

'I WANT ELIZABETH.'

'We know, we know,' said Sister Primrose.

'I WANT Elizabeth!'

The speed of the storm reduced. The heaviest pieces began to drop from the maelstrom, hit the floor and clatter into corners. Rosy crawled from under the table and joined the group. She squeezed Tara's hand.

'I ... want ... Elizabeth,' Tara said, fighting for breath.

Mona was in, holding Tara's arm. Sally came in, Rafferty and May.

The hurricane dropped. Mounds of debris drifted across the floor and settled.

Tara was completely wrapped up by the students and staff of Black Mountain. All that was left of the storm was a loose ring of dust slowly spiralling down. Everyone huddled together. They stayed like that a long time.

17

Ewan picked his way through the junk accumulated behind the warehouses. Among it, Akeem's home was well hidden. It was made of pallets tied together to make a cube. The inside was lined with cardboard. Andrew had given Akeem a pair of shoes and some clothes, they were in a tidy stack in the corner. Displayed on the lid of an old paint tin was a gleaming bar of soap. Ewan admired Akeem's creativity. These pallets were more homely than the Witness House. Akeem had made himself a place out of nothing. He was good at it, perhaps too good. He had escaped life on one city harbour only to settle in another. People stuck with what they knew.

Andrew was sitting in the opening of the house, doing something with his mobile phone. Akeem was next to him, untangling a fishing line he had found. Blondie lay sleeping in the sun.

'What have you been doing?' Andrew asked.

'Thinking,' said Ewan. 'What have you been doing?'

'Making,' said Andrew.

Andrew thought making was better than thinking.

'Still trying to do the right thing?' asked Ewan.

'He will help me stop the beasts,' said Akeem, glad to have an ally.

'I went to the library and found out what you are,' Ewan said to Akeem.

Akeem looked at him blankly. He did not want Ewan telling him what he was.

'You're an "unaccompanied minor",' Ewan went on. 'You came here alone and you're under sixteen. You're supposed to go to a police station and declare yourself.'

Akeem's lips made a worried shape.

'It's not bad,' Ewan explained. 'If you want to stay, the country will take care of you. You'll get some-where to live and you'll go to school. In London perhaps.'

'London,' Akeem said dreamily. Then he snapped out of it. 'First we have work to do. The eyepatch man brought more boxes in the night.'

Andrew had an idea and, to see if it would work, he was experimenting with his phone. He had opened the back, taken out the battery and prised open the inner casing. Next he lifted the seal over the phone's vibrator. Now he was stripping two short pieces of wire with his teeth. 'I bet Magee got a shock when he saw the mess,' he said between bites. 'He's spread the containers apart from each other. He won't be stacking them up any more.'

'There're fifteen now,' said Akeem, 'and more to come.'

'We've an idea to get rid off the dogs, properly,' said Andrew. He peered at the phone's tiny DC motor. It had a weight jutting out one side. This was the vibrating alert. Phones had several parts that carried current but Andrew thought this was probably the sturdiest. 'I went aboard the *Bounder* this morning and went down in the hold,' he said.

'Suppose one of the crew saw you?' said Ewan.

'I just would've said I was exploring,' said Andrew. 'That's what boys do right? Explore?'

'I suppose so,' said Ewan.

'There's a forward door in the bow,' said Andrew. He laid the two wires over the spring reeds of the vibrator motor before continuing. 'Akeem told me it can be opened from the inside with a push button. I wanted to try it. It worked and its electronics are very simple.'

Next Andrew draped a piece of electrical tape over the reeds and pressed it down. When he slid the battery and casing back into place the phone appeared normal but with two shiny wires jutting out. He set the phone to vibrate.

'Can I borrow your phone?' he asked.

Ewan handed it over.

'The *Bounder* is empty now and high in the water,' said Andrew. 'But with containers loaded it'll be a different story. The forward door will be half under water. I could see the hold used to have a wall in the middle, so there were two holds. If one sprung a leak the other would keep the *Bounder* afloat. But they've cut away the wall, probably because they wanted to carry massive long pipes or lorries or something. Now it's just one big hold. If the forward door is opened while the ship is loaded . . .' Andrew made a meaningful frown.

'We are going to sink the *Bounder*,' said Akeem.

Astonished, Ewan himself sank to the ground. 'What happened to dropping the containers off the pier?' he said.

'The containers would be easily lifted out of the water again. They might even float,' Andrew said. 'Even if they do sink we don't know the creatures will drown. May said they can't die. We have to sink the whole ship. And sink it out from shore.'

'The ship will be at sea!' Ewan said. 'The crew could be lost.'

'No,' said Akeem. 'We are saving lives.'

Andrew rang his own number from Ewan's phone. 'A ship that size will take a while to go under,' he said. 'Their lifeboats are sound. I checked them. Plus we can ring the coastguard before triggering the door. The crew will be fine.'

Andrew was holding the two wires between his thumb and forefinger but was not feeling the electric current he hoped for. He licked his thumb and forefinger and placed them over the wires again, water was a good conductor of electricity. He thought he felt a tingle but was not sure.

'*Trigger the door?*' asked Ewan. 'How?'

Andrew gave up with his fingers and opened his mouth instead. He pressed the wires against his tongue. Success. He felt the blunt pinch of electricity. Only two or three volts but that was enough. He held the phone up to Ewan.

'Mobile technology,' he said.

Ewan walked all the way to the end of wharf thirteen. Looking into the water he caught a glimpse of a seal curving up and under. As he watched the seal he heard a far-off diesel snort. Back down the wharf Magee was arriving with another delivery. No need to hide, if Magee saw him he would just be a tiny figure in the distance. Magee left the motor running while opening the warehouse door. He emerged in the forklift, took the red container from the trailer and brought it in. Soon Magee was back in the truck and gone.

Sixteen and counting.

Everyone had different motivations but the same goal. Akeem wanted to keep his country free of the dogs. Andrew wanted to do the right thing. Ewan just wanted revenge. He could not resist sending his father a text message.

'We are going to sink your ship', it said.

Ewan savoured the moment until it turned bitter. He looked at the mobile phone in his hand and was disgusted by it. It connected him with his father. He threw it as far as he could. It hit the water and drifted side to side as it sank away forever. Ewan did not hear it chime one last time, a reply from his father.

'You. Will. Not.'

18

When sorting out the school after the calamity, no one worked harder than May. She swept spilled food together for the compost heap. She hammered dented pots back into shape. She sawed broken furniture into firewood. Then she went looking for more jobs.

'Why don't you take a little break?' Sister Primrose asked.

'Don't want one.'

Sister Primrose directed May to mix a bucket of cement and use it to fill the gaps in the kitchen tiling. On her knees May trowelled it flat. The kitchen floor was smooth again but with big grey smudges. Not like a chessboard any more.

'When the cement dries we can paint black and white squares on it,' said Sister Primrose. 'Won't that be nice?'

In the sink May used her nails to scrape clean the trowel and bucket. She wanted the tools as good as new. Soon her fingers were raw and the palms of her hands wrinkly with soap.

Mona went by, on her way for one of her sneaky cigarettes. 'Why don't you take it easy for five minutes?' she asked.

May looked at the gleaming bucket. It could not be made any cleaner. Without warning she was crying.

'What's wrong?' said Mona.

The cries seemed to shake all the way from May's feet, she had to support herself against the sink. Her shoulders shook. Tears wrenched out.

Sister Primrose fluttered into the kitchen. She had radar for crying girls. 'Tell us what's wrong,' she said, stroking May's back.

'It was me caused Elizabeth to get sick,' said May between gulps of air. 'I was after fighting with Perpetua and was angry so I sat beside Elizabeth. She got in me head and made me feel better. But I must have got in her head too and she couldn't handle it. I'd so much badness in me—'

'No!' insisted Mona. 'That's not how it was—'

'IT WAS,' May spluttered. 'It was me badness that did it.'

Sister Primrose took May's shoulders and turned her. She looked into May's face. 'Now, you mustn't blame yourself. You're not responsible for Elizabeth's lungs failing.'

'I am,' May wailed, her face wet with released pain.

'No way,' Mona said. 'Elizabeth is not just disabled on the outside. She's like that all in her.'

120

Sister Primrose took over explaining. 'Elizabeth's disabilities affect her internal organs as well,' she said. 'She's very prone to illness. She's had pneumonia several times.'

'And her lungs have collapsed before, haven't they, Sister Primrose?' said Mona.

'That's right. It's not the first time she's been rushed to hospital.'

May's breathing was steadying. 'Her lungs collapsed before?'

'Loads of times,' said Mona.

May sniffed back her snotty nose. 'Maybe it wasn't me then so?'

'May, May,' said Sister Primrose, squeezing her shoulders, 'it definitely wasn't you.'

Mona allowed herself a little laugh. 'Nightmare,' she said. 'Have you been worrying about that all day?'

May made a damp shy smile.

'Now,' said Sister Primrose. 'Tea?'

'Save some for me,' said Mona, heading out the back door, 'I'm going for some fresh air.'

So, in the end, it was a good afternoon at Black Mountain. Elizabeth was recovering and would be back in a few days. It looked like everything would be all right.

Ewan walked into the living room of the Witness House. Andrew leaned in the door frame. Jones and Ewan's mother looked up from the television.

'I've decided you're right,' Ewan announced to his mother. 'I will support you.'

His mother was relieved. Too relieved to be angry about the time Ewan had taken. She stood and opened her arms. Ewan groaned internally. Did she have to go on like this? In front of Jones? He hugged her anyway. It looked like everything would be all right.

In the middle of the night there was a blast of extreme noise and Akeem jumped awake. He bashed his head on his roof. The back wall of the warehouse was still quaking from the detonation.

It was a bark.

A dog was out.

Akeem ran to a rip in the back of the warehouse. He could see a square of city light floating in the darkness; the warehouse door was open. Akeem saw a black shape, almost as tall as the door, run out through it. It sniffed the air, yelped joyfully then galloped away. The smell of death followed after.

The fat silhouette of the eyepatch man then appeared in the frame. He walked out on the wharf and watched the giant dog run. He had not delivered a dog tonight. He had released one.

On some evil mission, thought Akeem.

Akeem returned to his house and prayed everything would be all right. But he knew it would not.

19

Three in the morning. Identical houses on identical streets all held families in identical sleeps. Warm air drifted through the rose bushes. On Pine Street, white cats sat on car bonnets licking their paws. They looked like fluffy ghosts.

The drifting air sweetened, then bubbled into rancid stench. The cats cleared off. On the next street over, a car alarm began shrieking. With a rapid rhythm of dongs and gongs each street lamp was struck. Their tops rocked. Something was moving, fast. There was a crunch of a parked car being hit, then a snarl of frustration followed by a whistle rising. Over the rooftops came a car. Air whistled through its chassis as it flew. It had been knocked clean into the air. As it passed over, its wing mirror clipped a chimney pot. The car nosedived for Pine Street. It was going to be noisy.

CRUNCH.

The bonnet rippled. The roof crumpled. Every glass

part exploded. Compressed against pavement, the whole car shortened by several feet. It stood on its face a full five seconds before keeling over, *crash*, *bang*, *wallop*, into a garden.

A four-legged shadow charged across the top of the street. A yellow eye flashed and was gone. All along Willow Street street lamps swung as the dog glanced off them. It sheared the corner off a house as it swerved into Palm Street. A crooked tail, the size of a crooked tree trunk, snapped around the corner. The gable of the house collapsed into rubble. From different rooms a family looked up from their pillows and out on to the street.

It veered into a row of back gardens. Fences were crashed. Earth tossed up. Greenhouses shattered. The dog was thrilled with the hunt. Its tongue flapped from the side of its mouth, streaming tar. Sometimes, to its own ecstatic rhythm, the dog leaped. Three or four gardens were left untouched before it hit its stride again.

It slammed a chicken wire fence. Pressing on, the diamond pattern of the fence dug into its nose. Two posts were yanked from the ground, their foundations, globes of cement, dragged along. Two more were wrenched up. Six posts and thirty metres of fence were pulled away before the creature snapped its way through. It bounded up an embankment. Here it was bathed in tungsten light. Its black hair was slick, as if oiled. Its hunched shoulders were loaded with muscle, one higher than the other. Its body tapered away to a narrow stomach, taut and empty. In the centre of its yellow eyes the irises were contracted tight, giving the dog a look of electrified insanity. Its oily lips could not cover its teeth. The teeth were so large they were permanently bared.

The motorway was too wide to jump but the dog jumped anyway. It used a passing trailer as a stepping stone, but the trailer was being towed at sixty miles an hour. The dog's front paws were instantly whipped from under it. It flew in a corkscrew over the far lanes and struck the embankment. Momentum drove its muzzle through the soil. Then it was up and out of sight.

The trailer buckled. Axles bent and got wrapped in sheet steel. The noise was a deafening metallic yawn. Still contorting and folding, the trailer swung across lanes. Drivers of oncoming cars had to recover from the sight of the dog and steer clear or brake hard. They did not all succeed.

The dog vaulted off the embankment and onto a suburban street. It broke into another unstoppable run. Behind it, hubcaps and car doors shot into the air.

In his dream Andrew was climbing a tree. The leaves were bigger than life and kept getting bigger. Blanket-sized leaves began wrapping around him but it was not scary. It was comfortable. Soon Andrew was completely enveloped and was left hanging from a branch in a green pupa. He knew he would be a different person when he emerged. Then the dream changed. Green turned black. A night-dog raised its head and growled. When it barked Andrew woke up. It took a few seconds to remember where he was, the Witness House. Ewan switched on his bedside lamp and the boys looked at each other. They had never heard Blondie bark before. Then Blondie dropped to her stomach, locking herself into submission. The barks became long terrified whines, sharp as broken glass.

Jones must have taken the ladder in one jump. One second there was nobody. The next she was in the room, the spread fingertips of one hand supporting her crouched position. Her eyes darted about.

'Why would the dog bark like that?' she asked urgently.

'Dunno,' said Andrew.

Jones grabbed Andrew's T-shirt and dragged him over to Ewan's bed. 'Get down,' she ordered. Without hesitation she pressed them both down with one knee. She opened the clasp of her holster and drew her handgun. Finger on the trigger, she pointed it away in a neutral direction. She listened. Ewan, watching her from his subjugated position, felt an excitement almost as strong as his fear. Stars were twinkling through the open skylight, a billion miles away.

'Can you shut her up?' Jones snapped.

Blondie was whining. Andrew pulled her onto the bed and clamped his hands over her jaws. For an irrational moment he feared Jones would shoot her.

Stink poured in the skylight. More than a smell, it scratched the nasal passages. It was also familiar.

'My mother—' said Ewan.

'Hush!' said Jones. 'Stirling has her covered.'

A car alarm started screaming. The noise was more layered than the usual squeal. It was almost musical. This was because it was not one alarm but three, all set off together. Then the alarms were drowned out by the expansion of another noise. It rolled like thunder, along the ground towards the back of the house. Ewan's lamp vibrated across the locker and fell. Jones, the boys and Blondie were thrown as something big and blunt charged the house. Walls parted. Every angle folded. The bed tilted upwards as the floor bulged. They were forced to the wall.

The stink was overwhelming, like drowning. It reached down their throats and squeezed their lungs. Beneath them eight rooms were knocked into one. A hard ridge heaved side to side, fracturing the floorboards until they were detached ribs riding against the skin of the carpet. Jones pointed her gun at the shifting bump but did not fire. The creature's back was the only thing holding them up. Tar squeezed up through the carpet while hairs, each a foot long and needle-strong, punctured it. A few seconds later they withdrew, the creature had pulled out. The bulge collapsed. The bed they were on slid into the dip. The carpet was now a sack holding them above a two-storey drop. The creature bounded away and everything went quiet.

'No sharp moves,' Jones whispered.

Huddled together they listened, afraid of hearing carpet rip.

Choot, choot.

Not ripping. But what was it?

The tacks attaching the carpet to the edges of the room were pulling out. There was one *choot* a second, then four, then they came on like heavy rainfall. The carpet and all it contained was sucked through the middle of the floor.

During descent they had a brief impression of the carpet flapping around them like broken wings. The first floor was gone. Clinging to the mattress they fell all the way to the ground. The bed split against rubble. The carpet flopped flat around them. They looked up from a tangled heap.

The hollow space of the house was bigger than expected. Snapped-off beams jutted from the walls. Halfway up a toilet bowl hung grimly on. The washing machine was trodden down. The dining room furniture was flat-pack once again. A lamp stood primly in the corner of the living room, a freaky escape, it was still switched on. Everything else was mash.

Ewan staggered over broken bricks and fell to his knees. The remains of the house might collapse any second but he did not care. He tugged pointlessly at a torn radiator.

Jones was also overcome by sickening realisation. 'Stirling?' she said. Ignoring her own injuries she dug at the debris. Police cars arrived. Red lights flashed across the wreckage, making the place even more like hell. Andrew opened the front door to them. He seemed immune to everything around him.

'Leave him go,' a distant voice was saying. 'He's in shock.'

Andrew was sure he was not in shock, he could speak if he wanted to. It was just that time had slowed. He knew his words would only come out elongated and weird. No one would ever understand.

After dawn the bodies of Stirling and Ewan's mother were found.

20

Sprinklers whipped the grass to a lime-juice green. Between the lawns a tarmac path ran straight and pitch-black. It was a very orderly graveyard. Plots were slots where death was filed. The only messy thing was patches of tarmac melting in the hot sun. A sombre procession stepped around the sticky puddles.

Andrew and May stood apart from the other mourners. They knew nobody other than Ewan. Andrew listened to the oration. May listened to the butterflies. By the coffin Ewan stood with dry eyes and white knuckles. He had space to himself. The other mourners seemed bound to him but did not stand too close, like Ewan was a planet and they were caught in his orbit. Further out in Ewan's system policemen and social workers stood among the tombstones. They were sweating in black suits. In the far reaches newspaper photographers were using zoom lenses.

Newspaper headlines were screaming that dogs ran the streets again. Old people shook their heads. Just when things were getting good, they said sadly. Some gang had reformed and unleashed the dog, trying to destabilise the Peace Process. Police reserves were deployed in the city centre, they rode the streets in white armoured cars. Shops closed early or did not open at all. Politicians appealed for a return to normality. It was an isolated incident, they said, please go about your business.

'Akeem says Magee released the dog,' Andrew whispered to May as the oration rolled on. 'He works for Franklin. Ewan's ma was the key witness against him. They're trying to get the case thrown out of court.'

'If the house was secret how'd the dog find ye?' May asked.

'Good question,' said Andrew.

Even if Franklin discovered the location of the Witness House, how would you give an address to a monster? They could not fathom this.

'The dog went straight back to its container afterwards,' Andrew added. 'Container twenty-nine.'

The coffin was lowered. As Andrew watched he imagined all those containers going down too, sunk in the *Bounder*'s hold. He wanted them subtracted from the world just like Ewan's mother had been.

When the coffin hit bottom Ewan was walking away. The crowd, cut from their orbits, began to drift, but Ewan walked straight. Andrew and May followed.

Ewan walked through sprinklers. Ignored 'do not walk on grass' signs. Walked over graves.

'EWAN!' May shouted. 'Where're ye goin'?'

Ewan walked faster. Andrew and May geared up too.

'He's headed for the wall,' said Andrew.

Ewan broke into a run, towards the wall and its thick coat of vines. The wall itself could not be seen beneath the lush cascade of greenery. Ewan jumped, gripped vines in both fists and pulled himself up.

'Ewan!' May called. 'We're your friends!'

She and Andrew ran to the wall and looked up at Ewan. They caught a half-second glimpse of his hard expression, his mouth like a crack in a cliff face, before he dropped down the other side. Andrew and May grappled after him. On the other side was a sub-urban street. No sign of Ewan.

'He can't have just disappeared,' said May.

Andrew looked at the houses across the street. There was nobody to ask. 'He must have run around the back of the houses,' he said.

'I could ring him,' said May.

'He threw his phone away,' said Andrew. 'You go right, I go left?'

They split up.

Ewan hung until his arms gave out. He put his feet on the ground but waited some more before parting the vines and stepping into the sun. He brushed dry

132

leaves off his clothes and spat out twigs. That was close. Ewan was hidden only feet away when Andrew and May came over the wall. They could return any second and Ewan's social worker was probably looking for him too. He looked back at the wall. The graveyard had plenty of hiding places; he had already left Blondie tied up in there. He decided to climb back in until dark. A graveyard at night would not trouble Ewan. Ghosts were fine. It was the living he wanted to avoid.

21

After dark, Ewan, with Blondie at his side, was standing opposite the house he grew up in. It was the only house in the suburb without lights on. It had been empty for six months but this was not a homecoming. This was an investigation.

The spare key was hidden under its stone. The air inside was stale. Everything was positioned exactly as on the morning Ewan and his mother were taken into police protection. It had happened so swiftly. His father was only gone ten minutes when Stirling arrived. It was clear his mother already knew him. 'Ewan, we have to go away for a while,' she said, 'your father's been arrested.' That morning, standing in the kitchen, Stirling was solid and full of assuredness. He was dead now.

A coffee mug sat where his mother had put it down months ago. Ewan felt his heart creak in his chest. He reached out, touched the mug and looked inside. It was full of mould.

Now Ewan moved faster. He pulled two suitcases from under his parents' bed and searched them. Under his father's pillow he found his watch. He tossed it aside in disgust.

Ewan searched the attic and under the stairs. He dumped out cardboard boxes. He uncovered a long steel case. Was this it? The lid squealed on its hinges. Inside was only an innocent tool, a mechanic's jack with a long pump-handle. No good, he dropped the lid. He was looking for the Furies.

Ewan saw the garden shed from a back window. He went out and walked around it. Similar sheds could be bought in home-supply superstores but his father had built this one himself. All that effort and then he hardly used it.

The shed was locked. Ewan remembered the jack. It was a large, big enough to raise a van, certainly big enough to wrench open a shed door. He got it, lifted it sideways and inserted pedestal and base between the door and frame. He pumped the lever until the bolt ripped way. Inside was a lawnmower and a two-foot crowbar hung on a nail. Nothing else. There were no cavities in the wooden sides or roof. No in-between spaces where things could be hidden. He looked down. The floor was one large piece of plywood. Ewan tapped it. Hollow. Back outside he pressed down grass to see that the base of the shed was a sheet of aluminium, bent up around the edges. The shed had no proper foundations, it was just sunk a few inches in the soil. Between the aluminium sheet and the plywood floor was a small gap. Perhaps it was just to stop rising damp but Ewan wanted to know.

He found a screwdriver in the kitchen. Dozens of screws held down the floor. An electric screwdriver would have done the job in minutes, instead it took all night. After an hour, the tip of the screwdriver had worn away. It became rounded and kept slipping. Ewan leaned all his weight into each twist. His palms wore red. He cried from the frustration, the ache in his knees, the numbness running from his hands to his heart. More than once he exploded, grabbed the crow-bar and pounded the floor. It bounced off the springy plywood. The floor dented but did not crack. Ewan knelt down again with the screwdriver. Harder he worked.

I will know. I will know.

Dawn. Birds were singing. The last screw rolled away. From outside he lifted the floor. In the cavity beneath was . . . nothing. Empty space. He kept the floor raised above his head and stared at emptiness. It took time for his mind to accept what his eyes showed him. Nothing was hidden there and, judging by ridges of undisturbed sawdust, nothing ever had been. Eventually he dropped the floor, leaned back and rested his raw palms on the cool grass.

Now what?

Ewan was out of ideas.

It was when he walked around the shed that he got another.

By the morning light he saw a dip in the ground central to the shed's back. It looked somehow familiar. He ran his fingertips around it and realised it was the shape of the jack's base. Ewan got the jack and placed it in the depression. The pedestal slid snugly under the shed. Obviously the jack had been here before, many times. Ewan pumped the lever. With a puff of stagnant air a gap opened. Beneath soil level the shed's base was hinged like a trapdoor. Not just the floor or some part of the shed, the entire structure rose. There was a room beneath, lined in blocks, plastered and dry. When the jack was at its highest Ewan pulled himself under. He dropped to the floor of the secret room. He could almost stand up straight in it. The room was empty but for a dusty case in one corner. It was like a shoebox but longer and made of tough plastic. '*Honoris Causa* Incorporated. Ancient Solution to New Problems' was stamped on the lid. Below it said, 'Warning: Volatile Contents. The Furies™'.

In the padded case were six shimmering black syringes. They had long needles and tubes the diameter of rolling pins. The plungers were extended and ready for injection. So this was how the dogs were Furied. Ewan used both hands to carry a syringe into the light. He discovered the plastic tube was not actually black. It was transparent, the contents were black. Black, shiny and gritty, like sand after an oil slick. Ewan's eyes widened. The things inside were seething, shifting in their own strange currents. He held the tube close to his eye and saw it contained a hive of tiny maggots. They were packed tight and turning thickly amongst themselves. No food, no air, but the Furies lived. And they were his.

22

'Good morning, girls,' said Sister Perpetua.

'Good morning, Sister Perpetua,' they sang in unison.

Sister Perpetua took her seat. 'So, before we begin,' she said, 'would May like to identify the boy asleep in the guest room?'

Boy!?

The girls gasped so sharply the room was, for a moment, dangerously short of oxygen.

May went red and explained in a rush, 'We got back fierce late and Sister Primrose was away and ye were in your chamber and I didn't want to interrupt your meditating or whatever ye were at so I snuck Andrew in the guest room. I was just goin' to tell ye about him. He has nowhere to stay. It was our friend's mam's funeral yesterday but then our friend ran off and we spent all day looking for him but we didn't find him so we're goin' looking for him again today.'

'Are you indeed?' said Sister Perpetua.

'Aye,' May said before adding, 'If that's all right with ye.'

'First things first,' said Sister Perpetua. 'Go bring your friend down for breakfast. A boy who snores like that probably has an appetite.'

Soon May was leading Andrew into the dining room. She kept him close, as if to say, *he's my friend.*

'Let him take the end chair,' said Sister Perpetua. Andrew was sat directly opposite Sister Perpetua, next to Sister Primrose and Mona. The girls tittered and glanced.

'I'm Lizzy,' said Lizzy.

'Why don't we all introduce ourselves?' suggested Sister Primrose.

'I'm Rafferty.'

'Tara,' said Tara. 'Normally Elizabeth Dovell sits beside me but she's in hospital.'

'Green, Sally.'

'Rosy Motherwell.'

Mona dared to glance up at Andrew's chin. 'Mona Longley,' she said.

'And you can call me Sister Perpetua. We welcome you to Black Mountain.'

'Thank you,' said Andrew, on his best behaviour.

'Here we always start the day with prayer and porridge,' said Sister Perpetua.

Sally Green bowled up breakfast. Bread rolls were passed around. The food was simple and plentiful, just how Andrew liked it. He dug in and had second helpings. Everyone asked him questions. Mona imitated his Donegal accent. Andrew noticed she never looked him in the eye. Her hair hung down like a curtain while he talked to her.

'So, Andrew,' said Sister Perpetua. 'May tells us that your bereaved friend is missing and you're searching for him.'

'That's right,' he said.

'Your concern is commendable, but aren't such things better left to social services? Wouldn't it be sensible for you to go home?'

The girls went quiet to listen to this direct debate.

'Sensible maybe,' Andrew replied. 'But not right. I made a promise to Ewan's ma. I'm supposed to be keeping Ewan out of trouble.'

The girls were impressed by Andrew's dedication. From behind her spectacles Sister Perpetua pondered him.

'So be it,' she said, 'you may pass the nights here. But, Andrew, beware of keeping promises to the dead. They can never release you, can they?'

'Sure thing,' said Andrew.

General chat ensued once more. Andrew reached for another bread roll and noticed Mona looking directly at him. They locked eyes for an instant.

'There you are now,' he said.

Mona's hair fell like a curtain again.

*

141

May and Andrew went to the docks. Wharf thirteen was dry as a bone under the sun. The *Bounder* was silent in the distance. They found Akeem sitting on a bollard, fishing. He had a line but no rod. The lack of equipment looked ridiculous but as they approached they saw he had caught a fair-sized fish. It lay dead by his feet, its head bashed in.

'Have you seen Ewan?' asked Andrew.

'No,' said Akeem.

'He ran away after the funeral,' said May.

Akeem took the news with a slow sad headshake. 'When a boy loses his mother his moon falls from the sky. Trust me—' He jabbed himself with his thumb. 'I know.'

Akeem looked back to the water and began trailing the bait about. A fish was showing interest and he wanted it to commit to the bite. 'I hear the boxes will be loaded and the boat leaving two nights from now,' he said.

'We tested the idea with my own phone,' explained Andrew, 'but I can't wire that one into the forward door because if someone rings me the door will open too soon and everything will be ruined. But tomorrow I'll buy a new phone, so only we'll have the number, and wire it in. How's that?'

Akeem looked up at him and smiled confidently. He trusted Andrew and his work completely.

'I'm going to take a count of the containers,' said Andrew.

'Think I'll stay here meself,' said May. Even from this distance she could feel drumming on her mind. She would go no closer.

'How can ye be so sure the idea will work?' May asked Akeem when Andrew was gone.

'Because it is God's will,' said Akeem. He was watching the fish nibble at the bait.

'I'm not so sure there's a god taking care of us,' said May.

'He always takes care of me,' said Akeem.

He tugged his wrist. May winced. She slapped her hand to her cheek and felt the fear of an animal dragged into another dimension. Akeem pulled the fish up onto the wharf. It flipped and spasmed, wanting to coil itself up but impeded by its muscular thickness. May wished it could escape. Akeem reached for a piece of pipe to bash its head. Then the fish made a lucky leap. It flipped towards the wharf edge. Akeem dropped the pipe and grabbed the fish in his hands. Wet and powerful, the fish whipped out of his grip and bounced over the edge. It splashed back into the water and swam for its life.

Akeem leaped to the edge and bent his knees a fraction. He was going to dive but then thought better of it. A coin dropped from a ferry was one thing but nobody could swim after a fish. He turned and smiled sheepishly at May. 'God gives me what I need, not always what I merely want,' he said. 'One fish is enough for today.'

Andrew returned. He looked serious. 'Thirty-five containers,' he said.

23

Ewan was a fox, hiding by day and hunting by night. He slipped out and felt the darkness wrap around him. By now, he supposed, he was a reported runaway. There would be pictures of him on police station noticeboards. But Ewan had to go out and hunt. It was information he was hunting for.

How? How?

Once you had a Furied dog how did you direct it to a target? This was what Ewan had to know, more than he ever had to know anything. There was only one person to ask. Ewan hated him, he feared him, but he was going to Magee's house. Magee had no idea of all Ewan knew. He did not know Akeem had seen him release the dog. He might just give Ewan the information he needed. But it was going to be risky.

Using side streets and alleys Ewan crossed into a zone of tight-packed terraces. He found Magee's house but wanted to check escape routes before knocking.

Magee might not let him go easily. Along the back of the terrace was a service alley. It was littered with rubbish and sun-baked dog poos. Ewan counted the doors to the houses' tiny backyards until he arrived at Magee's. It was bolted but the wall was not very high. If Magee tried to block Ewan's exit he could run for the backyard, jump the wall and escape. He was glad he had not brought Blondie.

A glimmer against the curtains meant a television was on in an otherwise dark front room. Ewan tried to be calm. This was the moment before a car crash, drawn out in horrible slow motion. Magee's front door was unlocked. Ewan could walk right in but he did not. He stayed on the pavement and peeped in the window.

There was the man who murdered his mother.

Magee was in an armchair, empty beer cans scattered at his feet. The television was on but his chair was turned away from it. Instead Magee seemed to be staring into space, like he was brooding on dark thoughts. He was not wearing his eyepatch, a stream of tears was flowing down one cheek.

Ewan watched him cry a while.

Then he realised Magee was not staring into space, he was looking at the painting hung above the fireplace. The painting was of hunting hounds bounding through a forest. Red-jacketed huntsmen were following after. The painting was enormous, wildly out of scale with the room. The ornate gold frame was wider than the chimney breast. It would have suited a mansion better. Ewan noticed that the hounds were chasing a fox. They were about catch it and tear it apart. The fox had no chance.

Ewan stepped away from the window.

Need a better plan, he thought.

Teenagers were hanging around the bus shelter. Its backlit advertisements gave light. The adverts were for watches and health drinks, satisfied people looked out from under palm trees. They were semi-transparent. The fluorescent tubes behind them crackled, making their smiles flicker and hiss. The boys leaning against the adverts had shaved heads under baseball caps. The girls were unnatural blondes with big hoop earrings. They all wore tracksuits. Ewan was well out of his comfort zone but this was still a lot easier than facing Magee.

'Hello, Dan,' he said.

'Ewan?' said Dan, unslouching himself.

Ewan tried to make his mouth smile.

'How ya!' said Dan. He turned to his friends. 'Me and Ewan were great mates when we were wee.'

They signalled approval with grunts and squeaks.

''Ere,' said Dan, 'I hear your dad's up on charges. True?'

Ewan was glad Dan said that in front of the others.

It was no harm for them to know that, despite appearances, Ewan came from the tough half of the world. 'Yes he is,' Ewan confirmed, 'but he might be out soon.'

'Aye, well,' said Dan, 'my dad's been lifted a few times. They always get out in the end.' He leaned against the bus shelter again. 'And your mum? How's she taking it?'

'Not great.'

'Aye, well. What can ya do?' said Dan, sliding his hands into his pockets.

'I want to ask you something,' said Ewan. 'But not here.'

Dan got the message. 'Let's stroll, then,' he said.

They walked along by park railings.

'Our fathers made and sold killer dogs,' said Ewan. 'Giants. Did you know that?'

'Your dad hired mine to handle the practicalities,' said Dan. 'Storing them. Delivering them. That kind of thing. There were plenty of buyers. There was a war on.'

Ewan was impressed by Dan's familiarity with the business.

'Your father told you everything?' he asked.

'He's usually open with me,' Dan said, but so Ewan would not think he was comparing fathers he added quickly, 'He never let me see an actual dog. But I hear they get huge.'

Dan stopped and extended his arms as wide as possible.

Ewan watched disdainfully. 'They're a good deal bigger than that,' he said.

Dan dropped his arms. 'If you're so smart what do ya want from me?' he said. 'You were always like this ya know, snooty.'

Ewan looked at Dan. They were the same age. Once upon a time they were inseparable. If just a few things had happened differently then perhaps Ewan too would be hanging out in a bus shelter. He might have liked it.

'I apologise,' he said.

Dan smiled easily. 'Grand,' he said and they walked again.

'The dogs were made into giants by injecting them with things called the Furies,' said Ewan.

'Right,' said Dan. 'Dad says they've run out of Furies now.'

'I have the last syringes,' admitted Ewan.

'Ya do! Where?'

'Not on me,' was all Ewan would say.

Dan shook his head. 'Aye, well. Chuck them in the sea and the world'll be done with them,' he advised. 'The laboratories that engineered the Furies got destroyed. The Americans bombed them, part of their war on terror. Now your dad and mine are making more money reselling them. Some high-up people know the dogs are being shipped out but are turning a blind eye to it. They just want the dogs out of the country and don't care where they go. Anything to protect the peace.'

'There's one thing I need to know,' said Ewan, 'how do the dogs find their targets?'

'Your dad discovered dogs were the best animals to use. Dogs are trainable and loyal and . . . what else?' Dan was tapping his nose.

'They have a good sense of smell?' said Ewan.

'Right,' said Dan. 'That's how they're aimed.'

'They detect someone's scent across the whole city?' Ewan wondered aloud.

The branches of trees hung over the park railings, heavy with summer foliage. Dan ran his hands through the leaves as they walked. 'Even an ordinary dog's nose is a zillion times more sensitive than a human's,' he said. 'Giant dog, giant sense of smell. I doubt they'd pick up a whiff from across the country but a few miles, why not? Their sense of smell is what made the dogs such good weapons. Perfect for assassinations. You didn't have to know where your enemy was. The dog found them, did the job, then returned to kennel.'

'Or container,' said Ewan, his mind already working ahead. 'So, the dog needs a sample of the victim's scent . . .'

'Right, stick something carrying your enemy's scent under its nose. The Furies feed on aggression. They start hopping when their host is on a new scent. When the hunt is on they're unstoppable . . .'

Suddenly Dan reached up and tugged a handful of leaves off a branch.

'Those were bad days, Ewan,' he said eventually. 'We're too young to remember but our parents lived through extreme times. Now things are getting good but look at my dad. He's still half-traumatised . . . He used to keep things belonging to people,' Dan admitted. 'Things that carried someone's scent and were used . . . for jobs. He keeps them hidden behind a horrible painting in our sitting room. He doesn't know I found them.'

Ewan remembered the painting of the fox and hounds. He did not tell Dan he was outside his house only half an hour before. There was no reason to. This was still an investigation.

'He keeps them? Like souvenirs?' asked Ewan.

'More like memorials,' said Dan thoughtfully. Then he shook his head at the strangeness of it. 'What did I tell ya? He's half-traumatised.'

'What kind of things are used, clothes?' said Ewan.

'No, not clothes,' Dan said. 'Clothes actually aren't great at holding scent. It wears off too quick. Apart from gloves, they work well.'

Ewan thought about it. Could Franklin or Magee have gotten his mother's gloves somehow? Did she even have gloves?

'What's so special about gloves?' Ewan asked.

Dan held out his hands with fingers spread. 'Hands are the thing, ya see,' he said.

'Hands?'

'Hands are great for putting out scent.'

Ewan slowed. A weight materialised in his stomach. It was like a pebble, then a stone, then a brick.

'You need something that had plenty of contact with their hands,' Dan was explaining. 'That's why gloves are good. Or a watch. Or a ring— 'Ere! What's up?'

Ewan veered into the park railings. He grabbed on to them and dropped his head. Dan watched in concern. Eventually Ewan looked up. He stared in Dan's direction but did not see him.

'I am going to kill my father,' Ewan said.

Now it was Dan's turn to be impressed.

24

May and Andrew did not know where to look. Hardglass was so much bigger than their hometown. They looked in libraries and walked dozens of streets. May checked her mobile a thousand times. At dusk they gave up. They took a bus to Black Mountain. Rosy was by the door.

'Find your friend?' she asked.

They shook their heads.

'Mona's been moping about all day. I don't know what's wrong with her. Did yous have a fight?'

'No,' May said.

'Even Elizabeth coming back hasn't cheered her up,' Rosy said.

'Elizabeth's back!' May shouted in delight.

That morning Andrew was centre of attention, now he was left alone in the hall. He listened to the chatter coming from around Elizabeth in the dormitory. It was not a place for him. Instead he went outside. Broken kitchen equipment was stacked behind the school. Andrew pulled the casing off the smashed microwave and ripped out what he needed: two wires long enough to attach a phone to the mechanism of the *Bounder*'s forward door. He stripped their ends and rolled them up.

Andrew ascended the creaky stairs. Low-volume music came from under Sister Primrose's door. Candlelight flickered from under Sister Perpetua's. The hall was so dark Andrew even discerned candlelight in the keyhole. Quietly he went into his room. The electric light bulb was too harsh. Instead he lit a yellow candle stuck in a bottle. As he lay down soft light crept over the chunky furniture and the patchwork quilt on his bed. Andrew loved this room. It was full of peace.

Later, the knock on his door did not wake him. The visitor was not deterred. She crept in. She left the light off although by now the candle had melted down to the neck of the bottle and was breathing its last. The girl hovered over Andrew. She looked him full in the face.

'Wake up,' she whispered.

Andrew opened his eyes a little. 'Hello?' he said.

'It's Mona,' she said. 'I've been thinking all day, would I want to know or would I not?'

'Know what?'

'That time is *short*.' Mona clasped her hand over her mouth. Her nerve endings crackled. Looking into Andrew's eyes was heartbreaking but that was nothing compared to this unbearable decision. To tell or not to tell? Every boring day of her life she had no idea such decisions lay ahead. Mona wished she had known. Then she could have saved up some boredom and used it now to cushion her from this intensity. Yes, things could matter. They could matter a lot.

'Andrew,' she whispered, 'you're going to die.'

'We're all going to die,' said Andrew with a sleepy smile.

Mona's voice shot up. 'You're going to die, *soon*.'

She looked at him hard. The candle stump melted away and dropped inside the bottle. A final wisp of smoke drifted out of the neck.

'What are you grinning about?' Mona grabbed Andrew's arm and shook. 'You have family. People love you. Go spend time with them. You're going to die soon.'

That was when May crashed in. She knocked on the light switch. Andrew grunted and shielded his eyes. Mona shrank away.

'What do ye mean "soon"?' May demanded.

'I'm sorry!' Mona said desperately. 'I looked in his eyes this morning. I didn't mean to. It just happened.'

'What do ye mean *soon*?' May's face was crimson.

'May! Take it easy,' Andrew said, sitting up.

'What do ye mean SOON. This year?'

Mona was kneeling on the ground. 'No,' she wailed, 'this week.'

Crimson drained away and left May pasty-grey.

'Relax,' insisted Andrew, 'what does she know? I feel fine.'

Drawn by the yelling, Rosy came in. She squatted, concerned, down by Mona. 'What's wrong?' she asked.

'I caught her in here with Andrew,' said May, eyes locked on Mona. 'She's been using her Talent—'

'No! Don't talk about it,' Mona begged.

Tara and Sally were outside the door. Most of the school could hear.

'Do ye want to know what Mona can do?' called May.

'You promised!' Mona cried.

'Ye said ye didn't USE IT,' May shouted, full of what she thought was righteousness.

'Don't you dare!' Mona curled herself into a ball, as if by making herself small she could escape May's wrath.

'Mona says she—'

Suddenly May felt the texture of the carpet against her cheek. Stunned, she raised her head, wondering how she got to be on the floor. Tara had shoved her over. She was standing above May now, feet spread, arms folded, indignant and mighty. 'Don't say another word,' Tara snorted, 'you've no right.'

'If our Mona doesn't want us knowing her Gift then that's fine,' said Sally. 'We're her friends.'

Trails of make-up ran down Mona's face. Rosy had her arm around her. 'Most of us are, anyway,' Rosy said.

May ran from the room.

25

Ewan returned to his parents' house. The strip of Sellotape he had left over the door frame was split. Someone had been in. They might still be in, waiting in the dark. Ewan backed away and watched the house for a full twenty minutes. No glimmer. No movement. He went around the side. The Sellotape on the backdoor was also split. He scarpered to the back of the shed.

'Blondie!' he hissed.

Ewan heard her stand attentive. He had left her leashed under the bushes.

'Is someone in there?' he asked her. Blondie just wagged her tail. Ewan could have used May's super-power now.

Again Ewan watched the house. Nothing happened and eventually there was nothing for it. He went in and padded about, checking each room. Nobody. Whoever it was had been and gone.

The case of syringes was still in his backpack, under

his bed, untouched. With his hand inside a plastic bag he picked up his father's watch from the bedroom floor. He pulled the bag inside-out and now the watch was contained in it.

When leaving Ewan saw what he missed coming in. A handwritten note was pinned inside the door. It read, 'Ewan, please ring me. Jennifer Jones.'

Jones had come searching for him. Ewan pulled the note from its thumbtack and held it in his hand.

Jennifer, so that's her first name.

He had not known it until then.

Ewan dropped the note, stepped over it and left.

Furies heavy on his back, Ewan stopped to take one last look at the house he grew up in. Jones would return. He had to find a new safe house. He had two hours until dawn. He had a plan.

Soon Ewan was looking at another suburban house. His cold eye did not register the flowers and shrubs in the back garden. He saw only potential hiding places. Lamps were on upstairs but did not fool him. Aunt Sybil had gone to the caravan in Portrush. Ewan stepped through the clipped hydrangea to the window. He pressed the tip of the crowbar between the frames and, with firm pressure, the clasp sheared off. He was in.

Aunt Sybil's house was clean as a surgery. Rows of white plates stood on the dresser. In the semi-dark they looked like imprisoned moons. The kitchen was scoured and smelled like lemons. The bathroom smelled like roses. The slow tocks of the grandfather clock on the landing reached every corner of the house. Ewan chose the guest room for himself.

He led Blondie upstairs. While the dog sniffed at everything Ewan sat on the edge of the bed and took out a syringe. The needle gleamed, ten centimetres long, sterile but full of intention. The Furies turned in the tube.

'Come here, Blondie,' said Ewan.

He ran his fingers through the golden fur of her neck. She was relaxed until Ewan seized her collar. With his other hand Ewan lifted the syringe to Blondie's side. She whined and recoiled, her instincts said *danger*. The tip had not yet contacted her but the dog felt Ewan's tension. Perhaps she felt the Furies as well, close and seething with aggression. The syringe was awkward to handle. One-handed, Ewan tried to lock Blondie between his knees but she kept pulling away. Her eyes seemed to say, *Why?*

Ewan could not do it.

He let go and Blondie retreated to a corner. She mistrusted Ewan now but it was nothing a few pats would not fix. Ewan looked at her, at the industrial-sized syringe, and at her again.

Ewan could not do it. He could not hold Blondie and inject her at the same time. Both hands were needed to hold the tube and push the plunger.

She would have to be tied down.

'It'll be okay,' said Ewan a few minutes later as he pressed the needle into Blondie's side. Her front and back paws were tied together with strips of bed sheet. She whined miserably. Ewan pressed down on the plunger with his palm. Soon the plunger pulled away, sucked down from inside. The Furies only needed a push-start. Now they were driving themselves in, eager to invade a living body. The syringe emptied into Blondie.

Nothing happened for a few seconds. Then Ewan felt Blondie's body churn under her fur. She opened her eyes, they were yellow with pinpoint irises. Blondie snarled, a base note Ewan felt vibrate in his chest. Her bindings began to rip. Then she hit the roof.

26

The street preacher was attracting bigger crowds than the shops. 'Hounds of hell stalk the streets!' he shouted. 'Repent!'

The crowd quivered under his words.

'Ye should head home,' said May, 'it's dangerous here.'

'Drop it,' said Andrew. He turned away and examined mobile phones displayed in a window. He wanted a big blocky type.

May looked at Andrew's insolent shoulders. A thought dawned on her. 'Ye know ye might die and ye don't care,' she said.

Andrew walked past May, went in the shop and bought a phone. Outside he tossed away the packaging and inserted a SIM.

'We'll store the number in our own phones,' said Andrew. 'But whatever you do, don't ring it.'

'It's because of what happened last winter, isn't it?' said May. 'Ye saved me and Ewan but a man died and ye want to make up for it.'

'No!' said Andrew. 'I made a promise to Ewan's ma.'

'Only because you're desperate to do the right thing. Ye think ye sinned and have to suffer for it. That's the real reason ye promised. The reason ye won't leave. The reason ye want to sink those creatures. You're so desperate ye don't even care about death.'

Andrew was looking over May's head. 'Do you think I'd be able to buy electrical tape around here?' he asked.

'Aagh!'

May insisted in walking between Andrew and the edge of the pavement. She made him wait for the green man even when no traffic was coming. She steered him away from scaffolding. They were a long time reaching wharf thirteen.

'A complication,' Akeem reported. 'The crew are on the deck. They will see you if you try to get into the hold.'

They walked by the *Bounder*. Nine or ten men, probably the whole crew, were painting the walls of the superstructure, the tall part of the vessel containing the bridge. Most of the crew did not look much older than Akeem. They talked and laughed, their working pace relaxed. One man sat on a deckchair and was not working at all.

'We could wait until they go away?' said Andrew.

May kicked a loose bolt across the wharf. 'That'll be ages,' she said.

'What would Ewan do?' Andrew wondered aloud.

'He'd think up a plan,' May said.

Akeem furrowed his brow. 'I can do that,' he said.

'Andrew's not allowed to do anything dangerous,' said May.

Captain Marcus stretched out on his deckchair. He pulled up his T-shirt to expose his belly to the faint sea breeze. His crew were on maintenance duty. The *Bounder* was falling apart but a complete overhaul was beyond his means. A lick of paint would have to do. Captain Marcus looked towards the warehouse where his next cargo was stored. What was it this time? Cars, cigarettes, cough medicine? Captain Marcus did not ask. That was part of his service. He never asked.

The gangway bounced as someone ran up it. Captain Marcus raised his dark glasses. A young girl jumped aboard. She seized a life-ring from the railing and ran to stern.

'Hey!' shouted Captain Marcus. 'Those things are expensive!'

Captain Marcus pulled himself out of his deckchair. He was slowed by a limp; one of his legs swung out rigidly as he chased after the girl. By contrast his crew leaped like ballet dancers. The soles of their bare feet clapped nimbly against the deck.

'Me friend fell in the water,' the girl was shouting.

Captain Marcus was last to get to the railings. Below, a boy was struggling and gasping, obviously unable to swim. The life-ring was floating out of his reach, the girl had aimed it badly. The crew went into action. A youth stepped up to the railing. A fraction of a second later he was doing a twirl, nothing between him and the water but open air. He entered neatly and bopped up in the same spot. Above, a crewman tossed a rope ladder to two of his companions. In synchronicity they caught it, hooked the top over the railing and let the rest unroll. The bottom rungs splashed into the water. The youth pulled the boy to his chest and kicked back. The boy, almost lifeless, kept sliding from his grip and had to be reclaimed from the depth. The rest of the crew gabbled and pointed. How would they get the boy up the ladder? Another crewman stepped over the railing and into a high dive. The two crew in the water were able to raise the boy a little. The youth stepped onto the lowest rung, put his arms under the boy's armpits and hugged him tight to the ladder. On deck the others hauled the whole thing up, along with its two passengers. It was a tricky operation. Each rung resisted against the railings, clattering loudly as it went over the top. Eventually multiple hands manoeuvred the boy over the railing and lowered him on deck.

They knelt around him. His limbs were limp. His eyes were closed.

The girl broke into the circle. 'His name's Akeem,' she said.

One man pumped Akeem's stomach. Another gave him light slaps on the cheek. No effect. Captain Marcus pushed his way to the boy's side.

'I shall give him the kiss of life!' he announced.

That was when Akeem's eyes flicked open. He coughed and spluttered. The crew sat him upright. Water ran from between Akeem's lips as he grimaced. The crew looked at each other proudly, like a bunch of midwives.

'Thank you,' said Akeem.

'Are ye all right?' inquired May.

'Yes, yes,' said Akeem. 'I am okay.'

'I would have dived in myself,' said Captain Marcus, 'but I did not want to lose my leg.' He rapped a knuckle below one knee. It rang hollow. He pulled up a leg of his tracksuit to reveal that the leg was prosthetic.

'I think we can go now,' May said to Akeem.

'Yes. You should not be on these piers,' said Captain Marcus, serious but friendly. 'Go on home.'

Every hand pulled Akeem to his feet.

'And you should learn to swim,' said Captain Marcus.

'That is what I was doing,' said Akeem.

Hands on his hips, Captian Marcus threw his head back and laughed loud. In that unwary laughter Akeem was reminded of his entire country. He was almost homesick. Almost.

Andrew was waiting at Akeem's house.

'Done,' he said. 'I hid the phone in the casing behind the button. No one will find it unless they're really searching. I tested the connection. It works.'

'God is Great,' Akeem said.

'Those fellas seem grand,' said May. 'They saved ye, or think they did. Does their ship have to be sunk?'

'Sinking it is not just for me,' said Akeem. 'It is for the crew too, it is for every decent person everywhere. The monsters must die.'

'They're not one hundred per cent monster,' said May. 'The dogs are innocent.'

Akeem sniffed. 'Dogs are unclean animals,' he said, 'I do not care for them.'

May did not like that. Her eyes narrowed.

Andrew jumped in, 'If we could separate the dogs from the monsters we would,' he said to May. 'But we can't. You're still going to lend Akeem your phone, aren't you?'

'Aye,' said May after a pause, 'I was only saying . . .'

May gave her mobile one last loving stroke.

'Take May's phone in case we aren't here when the *Bounder* is leaving,' Andrew said to Akeem. 'I've already put the door-phone number in there. Ring the number when the ship is going out. You won't see much happen for a while but it'll sink. I promise.'

As if it were diamonds, Akeem wrapped the mobile phone in a piece of cloth.

'Thank you, May,' he said with a small bow. 'I will take excellent care of it.'

27

After dark Ewan went to the twenty-four-hour supermarket. He got in and out fast, the bright lights bothered
him. He bought food for Blondie, although he was not
sure she needed to eat any longer. Ewan had given her
four injections of the Furies. She had changed.

Ewan was on a cautious return route when a police
car cruised by. He lowered his head, but not suspiciously low he hoped. From the corner of his eye
Ewan saw a pale face and watchful eyes hovering
along the street. The police car disappeared at the next
junction. Relieved, Ewan took no notice of the neutrally coloured car coming the other way. Not until it
swung across the road. Ewan jumped. The shopping
bag fell from his hand and tins rolled into the gutter.
The car hopped a wheel up on the pavement, blocking Ewan's way, and the driver got out. Jones.

'Found you at last,' she said.

Ewan stepped back but Jones was next to him in a
flash.

'You've had me worried,' Jones was saying. 'Do you know Franklin might get released? We re-arrested him on suspicion of murder but we've no evidence . . . Are you listening?'

Ewan was glancing around and calculating. Jones had stayed in the car when Aunt Sybil mentioned she was going on holiday. And they were not near her house now.

My safe house is still safe.

I just have to lose Jones.

'Released?' said Ewan, to show he was listening.

'Ewan,' said Jones. 'Come with me. You've lost your mam and I think you're a bit crazy right now. I'll care of you, hmm?'

Jones's fingers squeezed Ewan's arms. He let himself be manoeuvred towards the car. Jones pressed him into the passenger seat.

'I want to get Blondie before we go anywhere,' said Ewan.

Jones was looking at him from the driver seat, smiling sadly. 'Where've you been?' she asked.

'You'll see when we get Blondie,' said Ewan.

Jones threw the car into reverse and they bumped off the pavement. Ewan directed their way through the suburbs.

'I want you to know that this is personal to me,' Jones said as she drove. 'I was supposed to be taking this week off.'

The houses tightened up. They drove narrow terraced streets, pulling over to let by oncoming cars. Jones was glad to have the task of driving to keep her hands and eyes busy. It made talking easier.

'Stirling was more than just a colleague to me,' she said. 'I cared about him a lot.'

Ewan could hear that Jones was upset. He watched the houses going by. 'Nearly there,' he said.

'Some people thought he was dull,' said Jones, 'but I thought he was consistent. Consistency is a good thing. And hard to find these days.'

'We're here,' said Ewan. They parked opposite a house with curtains drawn but light coming from the front room. Jones did not let go of the steering wheel.

'I was in love with him,' she said.

Ewan did not know what to say. He looked at the house.

'It never came to anything,' said Jones. 'Stirling was big on the institution of marriage.'

'He was married?' Ewan asked. From the corner of his eye he saw Jones' head sink towards the steering wheel.

'No,' Jones said. 'Me, I'm married.'

Even to Ewan's grief-numbed mind this cut through as a revelation. Not only did Jones have a first name, she had a life.

'It is possible to be in love with two people at once?' he asked her.

Jones was now resting her head against the steering wheel. 'No, Ewan,' she said weakly, 'it's not.'

They were quiet for a minute, then Ewan asked, 'Can you come into the house with me?'

Jones coughed and recovered her voice. 'Let's go.'

The door was unlocked, Ewan led the way into the front room. Magee was sitting in his armchair, eye-patch on, reading the *Telegraph*. 'Ewan!' he said, beginning to stand. 'Who's this?'

Jones already knew something was going on. There was no sign of the dog. Ewan turned his back to Magee and spoke to her. 'I need you to see something. It's evidence.'

'This is not usually how police work is done, Ewan,' said Jones.

'Police work?' demanded Magee.

Ewan threw the hunting scene from the wall. Multiple objects clattered against the painting's backing. They were in a dozen plastic bags thumbtacked in a grid arrangement. Watches, gloves, a cigarette lighter, and, in one bag, a pair of false teeth. Most of the bags were old and crinkly. Only one was fresh: a zip-lock bag containing a wedding ring.

'It was my mother's,' explained Ewan. 'This man used it to send that dog. The dog that killed her. And Stirling.'

'They're just keepsakes,' objected Magee. His eye burned. But Jones could see the collection was something strange and important. She knelt to examine the objects, especially the ring.

'You can't just walk in here,' said Magee.

Jones did not bother looking up. 'I was invited in,' she said. She eased off the bag containing the ring.

'GET OUT!' Magee roared at her.

Jones got to her feet. 'You'll have to answer questions about your possession of this,' she said, holding the bag out with a smirk. 'Isn't that right, Ewan . . . Ewan?'

Jones turned about the room. The door to the backyard was open and still creeping silently wider. Outside, she could see a wheelie bin was parked handily against the wall. Over it would be a service alley, a perfect escape route. Ewan was gone.

28

After noon prayers, Akeem went and counted the containers in the warehouse. Still thirty-nine, no delivery last night. Akeem placed one palm against a container. It was unpleasantly warm.

'That one's called Rex,' a voice said.

Akeem spun around. A man was sitting on top of a container. Not the eyepatch man, this man was wearing a suit and no tie. He looked like he had not yet made it home from a night out. In his hands, close to his mouth, was a half-eaten sandwich. He had paused mid-bite to watch Akeem walking among the containers. Now he sank his teeth in again. Akeem could not imagine eating with the reek of the containers but the man tore out a lump and chewed. He kept his eyes on Akeem.

'Rex,' he said again, 'as in Tyrannosaurus Rex. Do you speak English?'

Akeem did not say anything. He watched the man. The man watched him.

'Know a boy named Ewan?' asked the man.

Akeem shook his head.

The man chewed thoughtfully. 'Don't know him, eh?' he said. 'I'm looking for him. He's my son.'

Franklin gulped down the last of the sandwich and wiped his mouth. 'Rex was a Jack Russell,' he said. 'Just a little buck. The first dog I ever Furied. I'm sorry to say Rex's buyers didn't take great care of him.'

Franklin lowered himself down, dropped the last metre and landed on his feet. Akeem stepped back but Franklin was giving him a wide berth. He began walking between containers.

'Number two,' he said tapping a container as he went by. 'We stopped naming them after Rex. We just gave them numbers. Number two was a mutt. Had good teeth though.'

Akeem followed at a safe distance, horrified and fascinated.

'Number fifteen,' said Franklin pausing by another container. He patted it and shook his head. 'Number fifteen was a mistake.'

He resumed walking. The containers were set apart to stop them agitating one another. They formed a scattered maze across the warehouse. Franklin went in and out of Akeem's view. Akeem followed his voice.

'You are the man!' Akeem shouted. 'The man who made these monsters.'

'Twenty!' said Franklin. Akeem saw him step up to

the container as if meeting an old friend on the street. 'It came back from a job once with four bullets in its head. Four bullets! And it did not die.'

'Because it was already dead,' said Akeem. 'It is the beasts inside them that live.'

'It does stink in here,' Franklin admitted as he moved on. 'Even number twenty-nine is starting to rot. It breaks my heart.'

Akeem found Franklin with his arms stretched wide against container twenty-nine, as if he wanted to hug it. 'Twenty-nine was the finest,' he said. 'It was mainly Border Collie. You know, like a sheepdog? Not a vicious breed but twenty-nine came out just right. A big problem was always that injections of the Furies made the dogs crooked. Different parts got bigger at different rates. After a few doses some dogs couldn't even walk and had to be destroyed. But twenty-nine came out almost perfectly symmetrical. I wouldn't sell twenty-nine. I kept it.'

Franklin looked at Akeem over his shoulder. The boy was keeping well back.

'I owe my freedom to number twenty-nine,' he said.

'I know,' said Akeem.

Franklin set off again among the containers. Akeem lost sight of him but could hear him taking inventory. 'Eleven, thirty-one, twenty-eight, seven . . .'

'You are the creator of suffering,' called Akeem, scuttling after Franklin's voice.

'You can't pin that one on me,' Franklin's voice echoed between containers. 'The suffering was already there. It always will be.'

'You should beg God's forgiveness!' shouted Akeem.

'I'll see him someday,' said Franklin, 'we'll talk then.'

Akeem froze. Those last words had come from close behind. Franklin locked an arm around Akeem's waist and walked him up against a container. Akeem allowed his cheek to grind against metal, instead using his hands to protect the mobile phone in his pocket. A gurgle came from the container. The dog inside was awoken and riled. Franklin placed his free hand against the metal.

'REX,' he ordered, 'calm down, boy.'

They had done a circle and were back at Rex's container. Rex had not heard Franklin's voice in years but knew it in its contorted bones. The dog obeyed the tone of the creator and lay down again. It sounded like Rex was a smaller dog, able to shift back and forth inside his box.

'Now,' Franklin returned his attention to Akeem, 'if you wanted to sink a boat how would you do it?'

Akeem made a brave snort. 'Easy,' he said. 'I would pray.'

'My son will have a more solid plan. What've you got there, eh?'

Franklin pulled May's mobile phone out of Akeem's pocket. Now Akeem struggled, fighting to reclaim the phone. Franklin held the mobile up beyond his reach.

'Can I ask Ewan myself?' he asked.

Thumbing buttons, Franklin opened the contacts list. There were only three entries. 'Door', 'Andrew' and 'Ewan'.

'That's my boy,' said Franklin, 'but that number doesn't work any more. Who's Andrew?'

29

Andrew and May were on the bus to Hardglass. Andrew stopped mid-word, slapped a hand to his forehead and said, 'I know where Ewan is. His aunt was going on holiday. I bet he's hiding in her house.'

'Do ye know where it is?'

'It was only a short drive from the Witness House,' said Andrew. 'Let's go back and see if I remember the way.'

But the streets all looked the same and they walked all morning. In the end it was May's Talent that did it. She stopped and crooked her head. Andrew could tell she was receiving something strange but was hesitant to tell him what.

'Ye have to be careful,' she said. 'I'd go mad if anything happened to ye.'

Andrew smiled patiently. 'Mona says she's never been wrong,' he said, 'but wrong out of how many times? Hardly any, I bet. When we find Ewan you'll be able to take turns watching out for me.'

May hugged herself. From somewhere streets away a low throbbing came to her.

we . . . are . . . we . . . are . . . we . . . are . . . we . . .

'It's those crawly things again,' said May.

Andrew looked at the semi-detached houses all around. They looked harmless, boring even. It was hard to believe they could hide monsters.

'Where?' asked Andrew.

'Far off,' she said. 'I could find them though.'

She followed the beat as it became louder and louder. Approaching the house, Andrew recognised the severe hedging. Aunt Sybil's curtains were drawn so tight Andrew suspected they were pinned together on the inside, maybe with clothes pegs. Two windows were cracked.

'They're in a dog again,' said May with a shudder. 'The dog is alive still.'

'Is it frightened?' asked Andrew.

Digging into the Furies made May's stomach knot. Without realising it she was stepping backwards away from the house. 'Not really frightened,' she said. 'More like . . . heartbroken.'

They looked at the house.

'EWWWAN!' May shouted. No response.

'I'm going to look around the back,' said Andrew.

'I'm not goin' to watch ye getting ripped up!' May grabbed his arm but Andrew shook her off.

'Wait here, then!' he told her. 'Ewan might come out the front.'

The kitchen window was blocked with pieces of cardboard. When Andrew pushed one finger against the back door it fell in and crashed against the floor. Andrew waited for a response to the noise but nothing happened. The door had been smashed from its hinges and stood back up in its frame so the neighbours would not notice. Andrew stepped in. Every window was blocked, it was like being inside a package. Not just the door, the whole house was shattered. Walls were chewed open. The hallway carpet was ripped in long frustrated tears. The sitting room couches had been lashed at, their fillings puffed up into foamy explosions. Andrew stopped. He thought he heard a creak from upstairs.

'Ewan?' he said.

Shifting noises, then silence.

Andrew ascended. Upstairs, the doors had been knocked from their frames and the cavities bashed wider. Sets of parallel lines sliced the wallpaper and dug grooves in the brickwork. Andrew reached out and ran his fingers over them. They were claw marks, he realised. When he turned, a dog was looking at him from a bedroom. The dog was shaking all over, as if hypothermic. It shook so fast it shimmered, its edges blurred. The creature had the dimensions of a pony and the jaws of an alligator. The dog was so impossible Andrew's brain almost failed to perceive it. For a moment he saw through it, seeing only an empty

180

room. But there it was, an undeniable fact. Each tooth was the size of Andrew's thumb.

Andrew sucked in one sharp breath. He thought of Mona's warning as the breath rolled out again. He felt it pass between his lips. It was worth really experiencing this breath. It was going to be his last.

But the dog did not attack. It just stood there, simmering, every muscle overrun by compulsive ticks. It breathed rapidly, pumping a meaty smell into the corridor. Its eyes were yellow but for the black pins of its irises. Its fur was matted with tar but Andrew could see it was once the colour of straw.

'Blondie?' he said.

The dog's brain was saturated with the Furies but still recalled the name. Blondie barked and Andrew's eardrums clashed like cymbals, he would still be feeling that bark twenty minutes later. Blondie loped forwards, one of her legs shorter than the others. The floor creaked under her weight. Andrew tried to stifle his fear as she pressed the top of her head against his shoulder. She was a friendly creature.

Ewan emerged from the room.

'What have you done with her?' asked Andrew.

'Best to think of Blondie as *it*,' said Ewan. He looked tired and dishevelled, arms hanging like lead weights. 'The old Blondie is gone. I've injected it five times. There is only one more syringe to go. While it gets bigger it goes wild and throws itself about. As you can see, it's wrecked the house. But it calms down as the Furies settle in. Blondie was a good dog and this creature will do as I tell it.'

'But what will you tell her to do?'

Instead of answering, Ewan pushed his fingers through his hair unhappily. He fast-walked down the stairs and out the back door. After so long in the shrouded house Ewan was blinded by sunlight. He staggered across the garden and almost fell into Aunt Sybil's pond. Tiny insects were zipping about on the surface. He looked at them.

'You know what makes us different from animals?' Ewan asked as he heard Andrew approach.

'Dunno,' said Andrew.

'Revenge,' Ewan stated. 'No animal needs to take revenge. No caribou ever went after the crocodile that killed its calf. Or its mother. But we can. Sometimes we have to.'

'Better stuff separates us from animals,' said Andrew. 'We don't *have* to do anything. We can make choices. We're able to do right things.'

'I've already chosen,' said Ewan, 'and the dog's ready enough. I am sending Blondie after my father.'

Ewan bolted for the house. Andrew swung a foot out and tripped him. Ewan hit the lawn, rolled and sprang up again. Andrew was blocking his way. Face to face they stood for one heavy-loaded second. Ewan retracted one arm and punched Andrew below the collarbone. Andrew was surprised by the solidity of the blow. He landed on the grass, sitting upright. Ewan looked down on him, completely alive in the moment. He was getting a taste of why some boys love to fight. Then Andrew stood and hit him back, a proper boxer's jab that split Ewan's lip. Ewan tottered and tasted blood. Andrew had been in a lot more fights than Ewan. This was unsurprising, Ewan had never been in any. Ewan did have one advantage though. Andrew did not want to fight.

'Think!' said Andrew.

Ewan charged Andrew, bringing him down. With Andrew flat Ewan brought his knee down on his chest. Andrew made an *ugh* noise, pinned to the ground. Then his phone rang.

A truce. Ewan lessened the pressure on Andrew. The phone rang on.

'It's not me,' said May. She was standing by the hedge.

Andrew shifted until able to get the phone from his pocket. 'Hello.' He listened then offered the phone up to Ewan. 'It's your da,' he said.

Not believing, Ewan just stared. Then he snatched the phone and marched towards the back door with it. 'You're out,' he said, injecting hate into his voice.

'Free as a bird,' Franklin said, 'although I think the law will be after me again soon. The first thing I did was go to Magee's house. It's crawling with police.'

'Good,' said Ewan.

'You aren't really going to do anything to sink my boat, are you?'

'That's not going to matter in five minutes,' said Ewan. 'BLONDIE,' he shouted upstairs.

Lumps of plaster fell as she pounded overhead. She broke through the banister and, turning awkwardly outside the kitchen, smashed an internal wall. The Furies were gearing up for action and dragging Blondie's possessed body with them.

'What's all that rumpus?' said Franklin down the phone.

'An old friend of yours,' said Ewan, 'eager to see you.'

Ewan pulled out a drawer so sharply it whipped clean from its rollers. Franklin's watch, in its plastic bag, flew up and Ewan grabbed it from the air. Blondie barked and surged forwards. Ewan grabbed her by the collar, a man's belt, to stop her driving him into the wall. He shoved the watch under her nose. Her fur stood on end.

'Don't!' Andrew shouted. He tried to grab the watch but it was too late. Blondie was breathing in the scent. Her eyes popped. She shook as if electrocuted. The Furies pumped like jet fuel. At last, the hunt. They were bred for this.

'Listen, son, don't do anything rash,' said Franklin, coming to the correct conclusion. 'Let's talk.'

'NO,' Ewan screamed. 'Just be frightened!'

'Calm down, son.'

'Just be frightened!'

'Remember,' said Franklin. 'I've got your pal here and all my dogs to choose from.'

In the background Ewan could hear the slap and scrape of unlatching. A container being opened? The next thing he heard was Akeem's voice.

'Hello,' said Akeem.

Ewan straightened up. He pulled the watch from under Blondie's nose. 'Hello,' he said.

'I am meeting one of the beasts at this moment,' reported Akeem, a slight wobble to his voice. 'It has very bad breath.'

May and Andrew looked at each other. They might have made another grab for the watch but they saw that Blondie, just like Ewan, was cooling down. Her shake was slowing.

'I am avenging my mother,' Ewan said to Akeem.

'I trust Andrew will finish our work,' replied Akeem. 'So I am not standing in your way.'

With a snarl like one of his dogs', Franklin whipped the phone away from Akeem's face.

'HE IS standing in your way,' he said. 'Send Blondie and the last thing I'll do is have my dog bite him open. Call her off and I let him go.'

'We would all be better without you,' Ewan said to him bitterly.

May stepped forwards and took a hold of Ewan's arm. 'But we're better with ye as ye are,' she said.

'Let it go,' Andrew advised. 'Killing someone is the worst sin.'

Incredulous, Ewan lowered the mobile phone and looked at Andrew. 'Sin?' he said. 'Sin?'

The dust was settling from Blondie's ructions. Ewan dropped the phone and the watch and went into the back garden.

Andrew picked up the phone. 'You're safe now,' he said to Franklin.

Ewan was kneeling by the pond. He watched the insects skating about the surface. *They're so carefree*, Ewan thought, and then he shuddered at how low he had sunk. *Envying an insect.*

Andrew crouched beside him.

'Sin?' demanded Ewan, glaring at him.

'That's what I think,' said Andrew with a shrug.

Ewan looked back at the water. 'I don't believe in God anyway,' he said.

'Since when?' asked Andrew.

'Since I found out about monsters.'

30

Rex was standing half out of its container, juddering with excitement. Its grin was a metre deep. Its hide was like sausage skin, long and bloated but otherwise shapeless. The dog's contents sloshed about inside. Rex was rotted and blind by now. Its eyes were skinned over and streamed like greasy fried eggs. Its blood was coagulated ketchup. Its brain was mashed potato.

Akeem tried to look straight at its depraved expression. The dog leered back.

'We survive,' Franklin announced.

Akeem made a disinterested gesture with his lips.

'Aren't you afraid to die?' asked Franklin.

Akeem indicated upwards with his head. 'God is Great,' he said.

'Sure, God's fantastic,' said Franklin. 'But you're not. You're less than a speck. But aren't we all, eh? That's why we all have to find a small thing to do, and do it as well as we can. Let God deal in worlds. I'll deal in weapons. I've decided to accompany the dogs to

Africa myself, and I'm going to stay there. I've no role in Hardglass any longer. But Africa! It's a land of opportunity to a man like me.'

At that moment Rex snarled. The dog wobbled faster, its tail wagged so hard it fell off. The Furies were reacting to an intense anger coming from the boy, but on the outside Akeem seemed composed. He stood straight and self-contained.

'Can I have the mobile phone back?' Akeem said eventually.

Pointedly, Franklin put May's mobile in his own jacket pocket. The forward door's trigger had been taken from him but Akeem was unconcerned. He knew that Andrew would be on his way and they could use his phone instead.

'Rex! In!' Franklin ordered the dog, punching its nose to encourage it back into the container. He slammed the container door shut on it.

'Time for me to start loading,' Franklin said to Akeem. 'You can get lost.'

'It is you who is lost,' said Akeem.

Andrew was on his way, with Ewan and May. People who saw them screamed and cleared their path. Blondie was reeling along behind them, her jaws locked together in a massive grin. Crossing the suburbs they left a trail of screeching brakes, palpitating grannies and squealing toddlers. People photographed the dog with their mobile phones. Footage was on the internet in minutes.

In the city centre they passed the street preacher. He halted his sermon, raised a finger and pointed at the monstrous thing. His congregation turned and saw the dog too, accompanied, inexplicably, by three teenagers. The preacher's finger followed the beast's progress along the street until it was gone.

'The end is near,' said the preacher. He grinned, unable to hide his delight.

But Blondie wanted only to follow Ewan. She stuck close to him all the way to the docks. May and Andrew glanced back at the ugly loping creature. It was strange to think their friend had done this. Ewan carried the last syringe of the Furies with him in his backpack. It weighed heavily between his shoulder blades.

On wharf thirteen Akeem's eyes widened at the sight of Blondie. He scampered away and climbed a crane.

'It's okay,' Ewan shouted up to him, 'she doesn't bite.'

Down the quayside Franklin was forklifting each container to within reach of a crane. Crewmen leaped from container to container, attaching the crane's shackles then jumping to ground as they lifted. It was strange to see the graceless boxes sail smoothly through the sky. One by one they were lowered into the hold of the *Bounder*.

Loading took the rest of the day. Rays of the setting sun made the tops of the cranes glow golden. The vessel weighed deep in the water. Captain Marcus stood on deck. Via short-band radio he directed the crewman operating the crane. The *Bounder* was not built to carry shipping containers. They did not fit snugly, a gap was left up the middle, but they did all fit on one level. Captain Marcus ordered the containers packed tight to the sides of the hold. Even an unstacked load could shift in rough conditions and cause the *Bounder* to list. The smell also concerned him.

'My crew are troubled by this cargo,' Captain Marcus said to Franklin. 'They say they hear things moving inside. Do they contain goblins?'

'There's no such thing as goblins,' said Franklin. They watched the last container rise. Globs of black tar fell from it, dropped through the air and splashed on the wharf. All evening crewmen had danced around to avoid being hit by such drips. The hold floor was awash with foul soup.

'I might have refused to carry this strange cargo had you not requested to travel with us,' Captain Marcus said to Franklin. 'I take your presence aboard as guarantee the cargo is safe. A man might conjure demons, but he would not go to sea with them.'

'He would have to be desperate,' said Franklin.

'Do you like your cabin?' asked the captain.

'Yeah,' said Franklin, 'I've always been fond of rats.'

Captain Marcus's loud laughter rolled out like a wave. Then he pointed towards one of the thick ropes mooring the *Bounder* to the quayside. 'Rats will not be a problem,' he said. 'They do not like your cargo either.'

A dozen rats were scarpering down the rope, onto the wharf and away, abandoning ship.

The engine limbered up for departure. The propeller spun, chopping water up white. Crewmen wound in the moorings. The freighter groaned away from the wharf and towards the open sea.

Akeem, Ewan, May, Andrew and Blondie walked along the wharf in silence. The quayside was patterned by black rectangular outlines, left by the leaking containers. They watched the freighter get smaller as it ploughed towards the dark horizon.

'Do you want to do it, Akeem?' said Andrew.

'Can I?' asked Ewan.

Akeem deferred to Ewan. With grim satisfaction, Ewan took Andrew's phone.

May chewed her lip. 'It's a fierce thing to do,' she said.

'It'll cause a fierce amount of murder if it's allowed to go,' said Ewan. 'Besides, I am not letting *him* escape.'

May turned away. She felt the seals drifting sleepily among wharf supports beneath her feet. She focused on them. They were the only innocent things around here.

Ewan pointed the phone towards the freighter as if it was a remote control. He pressed 'call'. They could hear the ringtone but then it cut and a voice said, 'Good evening!'

'Oh no,' said Andrew.

Franklin chuckled down the line. The roaring engine and loud rush of sea could be heard in the background. He was on the deck of the *Bounder*.

'Seeing the word "door" in the boy's contacts got me thinking,' said Franklin. 'Before loading I checked the forward door. That was a clever bit of wiring. Might have worked, if I hadn't pulled it out.'

Ewan's body sagged. Unable to address his father directly, he closed his eyes and said, 'No, no, no.' Ewan might have sent Blondie right then but he had nothing carrying Franklin's scent. His father was getting away with his freedom, with the dogs and with murder.

'I'm impressed by your try,' said Franklin. 'I'm proud, in a way. There's only one thing left for me to teach you about: disappointment.'

Wind whistled through the earpiece, then the swoosh of immersion. Franklin had thrown the phone in the sea.

Akeem was also learning about disappointment. He felt his faith shake then collapse. The freighter was going to his homeland with a cargo of war and chaos. No intervention had stopped it. Without announcement, Akeem stepped out of the shoes Andrew had given him and walked to the edge of the wharf. He dived.

'AKEEM. COME BACK,' shouted May.

Already ten metres out, Akeem broke the surface swimming a sleek front crawl.

'He'll never make it,' said Andrew. 'The ship's too far. Nobody swims that fast.'

'He's gone insane,' said Ewan.

'Noooo!' May wailed. Then something occurred to her. She looked and saw Andrew already had one shoe off. May jumped and looped her arms around him. Locked together they fell. May banged her head against the wharf but did not let go.

'YE are goin' to LIVE,' she said. 'Akeem's a way better swimmer than ye. Let him go.'

Andrew went limp and watched Akeem swim away into the dark wake of the *Bounder*. May pressed her head into the back of his neck and closed her eyes tight. She was terrified for Akeem, for Andrew, maybe for the whole world. 'Let him be all right, let him be all right,' she kept repeating. She would not have known if she was saying it out loud or just thinking it. She cared for nothing else. 'Let him be all right, let him beallright, *lethimbeallright* . . .'

Beneath, the seals twitched.

31

Akeem would not waste energy on prayer. There was only the swim. He *was* the swim. He was the push, the lift, the slice. Each reach reached only as far as it had to, no more. Every cut, every twist, and every suck of breath, everything had to be perfect. One falter, he told himself, and he would be lost. He told himself and he told himself until his every fibre knew it. Then he put his brain on standby.

Push. Lift. Slice. Push.

No need to look back to know wharf thirteen was out of sight. No need to look forwards to know he was in the wake of the *Bounder*. He could hear its engine, taste its oily trail and feel the way the water was churned and broken. There were ladders recessed into the hull. Reach one and he could get aboard.

Push. Lift. Slice. Push.

The water became stiffer. The surface rippled with slappy waves. Akeem had broken the boundary between two currents, he was beyond the city harbour and into solid sea. Still he did not pray.

Twenty minutes he swam.

Push . . . Lift . . . Slice . . . Push . . .

Breathe.

Now the *Bounder*'s wake was resealed by the time Akeem reached it. The engine noise was disappearing into the waves.

Push . . . push.

Breathe.

Akeem could not hear the boat any more.

Exhaustion reached from the deep and gripped him mightily. His arms seized up, his legs were clamped in water. He brought his head up. Over the black waves the stern of the *Bounder*, an upside-down triangle, was shrinking. It was too far ahead. The docks too far behind. Sky above and sea below extended on for ever.

Breathe.

Akeem felt the depth of the sea as a heaviness, a weight somehow bearing down on him from below. He was a speck in the void.

Breathe.

There is a time where no human mind is strong enough to do anything but panic. That time was soon.

Still Akeem did not pray. Instead he thought this: the world's seas are all linked. The seas and oceans all turn in one vast body of water. Eventually every part touches every shore. Akeem decided he was not dying so far from home after all. We all swim the same water.

Something slipped by Akeem's wrist. Maybe it was death itself, checking his pulse. Seconds later it collided with the back of his legs. Akeem's head dipped under but was propelled back up as quick. Something had lifted him. It was slippery and fast, more fluid than the hard sea it cut through. Not just one, a pack of living things pressed around him, nudging and cajoling. One bobbed up and regarded him with wet pebble eyes. Akeem's senses returned but still could not make sense of this. They were seals. Lots of them.

The seals turned beneath Akeem, rolling and turning and carrying him across the surface. At first he splashed and gasped, disbelieving. When he accepted their support and threw his arms back the seals accelerated. Akeem skimmed the water. There were dozens of seals turning in a tight corkscrew beneath him. Each bore Akeem forwards only momentarily before swerving off and being replaced by the next. Their speed dazzled him, and then they got faster. They were carrying him to the closest high ground available.

The freighter was ponderous and brutal compared with the grace of the seals. But it was massive, a mountain in movement. Heavy-loaded, it cut steady through the shifting waters. The blunt bow bulldozed the sea apart. Akeem was brought in a wide arc towards the *Bounder*'s side. They hit the two-metre swell of the freighter's displacement, tonnes of water turning over in an endless furrow. The swell snatched Akeem up from the seal's backs and dropped him again. The seals had to increase their rhythm, drilling harder and harder to bring the boy to the boat. Avalanches of water worked against them. After only a second under Akeem each seal was sucked away. He saw two seals, then four, twirl away in the wash, exhausted and helpless. After a world of water it was a shock to Akeem's system when he smacked into the steel cliff of the *Bounder*'s side. He was tiny against it, a fly hitting a windscreen. Then the steel plates of the hull were rushing by, as if the freighter's speed had boosted. But it was not going any quicker. Akeem was now in the fastest part of the *Bounder*'s wake and being speeded towards the propeller. A seal shot from under him and bounced to stern. It had no chance. Akeem drove his palms against the racing hull. Rivet heads sliced the skin of his fingers. The instant he felt a ladder he locked down on it. His legs yanked from under him and he was laid horizontal into the wash. Akeem clung on, swallowing seawater. *Up*, he told himself. *One hand at a time.*

Two rungs. Three—

One seal, fighting the spill, watched Akeem for a few seconds. Akeem saw its clever whiskers and gleaming eyes before it went under and away. Akeem's heart fluttered in disbelief. Seals!

He flipped over the side and landed on his back. Despite the possibility of being seen from the bridge Akeem lay still a while. The deck, still warm from the day's sun, felt pleasant through his shirt but his mind reeled. It had happened. God had reached out and saved him with seals. God was Great.

Wharf thirteen had the grim atmosphere of defeat. Ewan and Andrew sat slumped. May was walking back and forth. Her anxiety for Akeem was turning into anxiety for Mona. They had not spoken since their fight. May felt the exhausted seals return from somewhere but did not give them much attention. She had not even realised they had been gone. May had sent the seals after Akeem without being aware of it. When needed her Talent grew powerful enough to make the seals act. Her concern for Akeem flowed into them as clear as any stream. It had carried them away.

But May would never know her Talent saved Akeem. He would never know it either.

Akeem felt the freighter's deck vibrate with engine power. It was the *Bounder*. It was a general cargo coaster. Forty years old. In its time it had been a South African coaler, a Mediterranean roll-on trucker, a cargo ship hauling figs to France. It had a one-thousand-horsepower engine, was sixty metres long and had a displacement of two thousand five hundred tonnes. It was carrying thirty-nine monsters to Nigeria.

Akeem stood. He was Akeem Murtala Mohammed. He was a Lagos dock kid. Fourteen years old. He had been a student, a barrel cleaner, a fish-gutter, a son and a brother. He was less than five foot tall and lightweight. He was going to sink the *Bounder*.

32

Akeem dived into a ventilation shaft. He bounced down, his palms slapping off the sides to slow his descent. Out of the tube he fell through open air. He tried to make his body loose while his instincts revolted. He had nearly died escaping this hold and now he was deliberately throwing himself back in. It felt like many seconds before he hit a container top. He waited for pain. None, or at least not too much. No bones broken. Some light entered through the shaft, Akeem could see the containers waiting in rows.

He ran along their tops. At the bow he stopped and stared. Containers were stowed tight to the wall. Immovable. The button was blocked away and out of reach.

Nooo.

A worst-case scenario turned over in Akeem's mind. The monsters would be delivered. The *Bounder* would return to Lagos and he would just be a foolish stowaway, accidentally returning to where he had come from.

Allah, thought Akeem, *it is me again*.

An alley ran between the containers all the way back to the engine room bulkhead. Their doors faced in at each other. Some were padlocked but some were just latched shut.

Thinking it and trying it were the same thing.

Akeem took a deep breath and lowered himself down. Breaking the skin of the swamp released a new cloud of putridity. Rotten stew oozed between Akeem's toes and up his ankles. He held his breath as long as he could before the inevitable gasp. He unlatched a container door. Then another.

Akeem had already unlatched nine or ten containers before anything happened.

A screech cut into his eardrums. No dog could make such a noise. A creature the size of a cow slid out of its container in a wave of its own gunk.

What?

It was a rat. It stood on its hind legs, forehands spread against each side of the alley. It sniffed the air with loud nasal suctions. Akeem backed away. He had banked on released dogs not attacking him but this was unexpected. What would a Furied rat do?

It dropped to all fours and charged at him, that was what.

'Aaah—'

201

The next container door shot open, pinning the rat's neck against the opposite container. Even as it struggled the giant rat kept its yellow eyes on Akeem.

Annoyed by the noise of the rat, number eleven had headbutted out. It was almost a relief to see it was a dog. The creature had the erect head of a hound. Milky slime leaked from its ears. It was once a German shepherd but was now a gigantic hairless perversion. It looked at the trapped rat. Then it looked at Akeem.

'It was I who released you!' Akeem tried to sound assertive as he opened other containers. Three, nineteen, twenty-seven . . .

Twenty-nine's container exploded with rage as soon as it had vent. A massive shock wave rippled through the hold. Rivets shot off as it peeled back its container roof. Twenty-nine squeezed out and stood atop the containers on splayed legs.

Time to hide. Akeem was completely out of scale with the nightmare he had created. He dived down a narrow gap next to the hold wall. He felt the *Bounder* lurch as the creatures emerged from their containers and began to battle. A fury of teeth, claws, and breaking bones rolled around the hold. Then Akeem stopped thinking and experienced the perfect clarity of extreme terror. The rat was squeezing down with him. Akeem saw every whisker in the rat's face and felt its tarry fur run over his hand. The rat was not chasing Akeem. It was trying to hide too, clawing desperately downwards. Its tail flopped and folded into the gap and draped across Akeem's shoulders.

Akeem once had a job assisting a snake charmer who worked the streets for money. Part of Akeem's job was walking around the gathered crowd with a thick rock python, encouraging people to pet it. Akeem would carry the snake over his shoulders. The rat's tail felt just like it.

The rat screeched and reversed. Actually it was being dragged, claws were dug in its hindquarters. Akeem could see the yellow headlamps of a different creature. What had those men been thinking? It was a cat. Its mouth was a pus-filled bear trap. It hissed and its back arched with the pleasure of the kill.

MEEEAAAAAA—

Gruuuf.

The cat's eyes widened in trauma. Black blood hit the hatches. A set of jaws had clamped down on it. The dog yanked, dragging both cat and rat away across the container tops. It was twenty-nine. It ruled the hold.

The rat's tail whipped away after it. Akeem saw the hatches above were opening, revealing stars.

My chance . . .

Akeem seized the end of tail and let it catapult him up. He soared. As he shot above deck Akeem glimpsed the crew's horrified faces, looking down into the hold. Then he saw the tops of their heads. Then all he saw was sea.

A hand, on the end of an outstretched arm, caught Akeem's ankle and snapped him back. As soon as he hit deck he was roughly lifted. Crewmen stepped aside as Akeem was shoved to the edge of the hold. It was a war pit. Rats, cats, but mainly dogs, every monster snapping at every other.

The hands on Akeem belonged to Captain Marcus. 'What are these . . . these . . . ABOMINATIONS?' he demanded.

'It is *your* cargo,' said Akeem. 'You are the one taking them home.'

A collective *whaaa* went up from the crew.

Captain Marcus raised his hands in a gesture of helpless ignorance. 'I did not know,' he said. 'Why were you among them?'

'I wanted to open the hold and drown them.'

Another *whaaa* went up.

'The arms trade is a legitimate trade,' Franklin said coolly. He had come out of his cabin and was stood among them. The crew recoiled from him, this master of monsters. 'I see my cargo is causing a rumpus,' he said to Captain Marcus. 'Don't worry, I'll get them back under control, and I'll increase your payment ten per cent in compensation for the mess. Agreed?'

Captain Marcus looked into the hold. Two dogs, locked together, bounced against the sides. Others were backed into corners and snarling. Akeem recognised Rex. It had been attacked and was heaving itself along on its front paws, dragging its torn body behind it like a burst water balloon.

'You would bring these things to your home?' asked Akeem.

'We can change destination,' Franklin offered. 'Somalia maybe. Or Sudan.'

One of Captain Marcus's eyebrows arched into his forehead. 'I'm from Sudan,' he said.

Franklin sighed at how childish this was becoming. 'Then you'll understand the need for a defence trade,' he said. 'These are weapons. I'm exporting them. I can do it with the *Bounder* or charter a different boat. Either way it gets done.'

Captain Marcus looked at his crew. They watched him expectantly. He looked up to the bridge. The faces of other crewmen were pressed against the glass. Captain Marcus signalled that they close the hatches.

'I'll go down and sort out the dogs,' said Franklin.

'No, I would not go down there,' said Captain Marcus. 'It is about to get very wet.'

The crew jumped to it, running to prepare the lifeboat. Captain Marcus left for the bridge, from where he would scuttle the ship. Franklin took it calmly. He did not even glance at Akeem as he stuck two of his fingers in his mouth and whistled.

'Twenty-nine. HEEL!'

Twenty-nine knew its master's voice. It leaped up against a closing hatch. Two assaults and the hydraulics splintered. One more and the dog was out. The hatch hopped before crookedly slamming shut, billowing air across deck. The dog wobbled to starboard, causing the *Bounder* to pitch.

'Easy boy, easy,' said Franklin.

Franklin could see the dog was about to bark. He covered his ears.

The blast fractured the bridge windows into webs of white lines. Captain Marcus was not distracted. Flicking switches, he cut the fuel to the engine, opened the ballast tanks and the forward door. At the stern the lifeboat dangled out over the water and crew were swinging into it. The lifeboat was not slung straight but the rigging was not the problem. The *Bounder* was already wallowing to bow. Every horizontal was sloping and would soon be sucked under. Captain Marcus saw the stowaway. The boy had his arms out, trying to balance, and was obviously sick with apprehension. It was hard for a mind to accept that what was now so solid would soon be gone. All this would soon be open sea.

Akeem went to clamber onto the lifeboat but Captain Marcus had no patience for that. He lifted the boy up and tossed him into arms of his crew. 'Everybody in?' he shouted.

The propeller broke the surface as the bow went under. Now the freighter's momentum drove it into the sea instead of over it. A chain of glowing portholes slid under at a thirty-degree angle. From a distance they looked like dying stars, fizzling out one by one.

A small sample of two-thirds of the earth's surface was gushing into the hold. Loose creatures fought until drowned but many of those in their containers would survive the sinking. They did not need air. In fact, lack of air preserved them. They felt the chill as their containers submerged. The creatures would be held decades more by the containers, by the hull and the whole sea above. They would wait until their bodies finally fell apart. Then the Furies, without hosts, would wait for evermore.

Franklin stood in the middle of the deck, about to be inundated from both sides. Twenty-nine simmered and shook. The dog was far taller than Franklin but kept its head low in subservience.

'Good boy,' said Franklin. 'Good boy.'

From the corners of both eyes Franklin saw water foaming. The deck lurched under and sea rushed to meet itself. Twenty-nine flinched as water washed around its ankles. Franklin's voice calmed it.

'Good boy, good boy.'

33

Ewan and Andrew sat on wharf thirteen. May was gone. She said she had something to do back at her school, something that could not wait. She directed Ewan to keep a close watch over Andrew before leaving.

Andrew held open Ewan's backpack and looked at the last tube of Furies.

'Just throw it in the sea,' said Ewan. His chest heaved as he looked back at Blondie. Even in her sleep she tremored.

A blunt sound pounded the sky. The boys had it identified as a helicopter before it flew over the warehouses. Ewan had rung Jones but she said nothing about coming in a helicopter. It was not Jones, of course, it was air-sea rescue. It powered overhead and out to sea.

Ewan looked at Andrew.

'There's no way Akeem caught the ship,' said Andrew. 'Forget it.'

The helicopter roved over the horizon. Its spotlight picked out a lifeboat. Men's backs were leaning into oars. The crew of the *Bounder*.

'Look!' said Ewan.

'I don't believe it,' said Andrew, 'the *Bounder* must be sunk.'

'Yes, but I am not talking about that. Look there!'

Nearer than the lifeboat, Andrew saw the flash of a yellow eye. A dog was swimming for wharf thirteen. A man was riding on its back. His fists gripped tufts of the dog's neck hair and his knees locked hard to its sides.

'My father,' said Ewan.

'Do you want to hide?'

'No.'

Soon, twenty-nine jumped onto the wharf. Franklin dismounted and retreated underneath the wet dog. He knew what came next. Twenty-nine shook itself, a muscular twist that began at the shoulders and ran to the rump. Flurries of hard rain lashed right and left.

'As I was saying,' Franklin said, coming out from under the dog, 'I'm proud, in a way.'

Blondie sat up and growled at him. Ewan held his hands together and looked at his father. He did not need to say anything.

Sirens were approaching. The police.

'I must get this dog away from me,' said Franklin. 'And those blacks have wronged me terribly.' Franklin reached into his pocket and pulled something out. The boys knew the object was a threat to someone because it was in a zip-lock bag. But it was too late. Franklin already had the mobile phone under twenty-nine's nose.

Twenty-nine electrified. Its eyes bulged. Its hair stood on end. Furious joy exploded within and the dog reared. A chase. A hunt. It flinched its way along the quayside, barked at the lifeboat but did not dive. Instead it turned from the sea and sniffed the air. Franklin wondered what was delaying the dog. The mobile had been taken from the African boy, had it not?

Andrew looked at Ewan but managed only one word. 'May.'

Franklin took the phone from Akeem but he had had the phone only a short time, and had barely touched it at all. It was May who loved the phone, her link to her friends. It was May's scent the phone was carrying. And it was after May that the dog was going.

Twenty-nine sprang into a run. Headed for the city.

'Blondie!' yelled Ewan. He gestured madly after the running dog. 'Get it!'

Blondie barked and hurtled after twenty-nine. From the other direction a police car came screaming down the wharf. Jones was following behind. They stopped in a V formation with Franklin in their headlights, cornered but composed. Ewan threw himself in the front passenger seat of Jones's car. There was no time to waste.

'Dog,' he said, pointing. 'After our friend. Black Mountain. GO.'

Jones got it. They streaked off. Andrew was thrown across the back seat and hit the window.

'Seat belts,' Jones advised.

Outside the docks they saw parked cars with bashed-in bonnets. Jones followed a trail of destruction. They raced under a concrete overpass and towards the city centre.

'No, that way!' Ewan was shouting and pointing.

He had just see Blondie overhead on the motorway. Actually she had been above it, thrown, it seemed, into the air during a fight. They could hear her barks as Jones swerved across three lanes to catch the slip road. The car hit an oil patch and went skimming sideways. Signposts, the motorway, even the stars in the sky raced by in a blur. Jones mouthed noises like *fa fa fa* while dragging the steering wheel around. The tyres clawed the surface, grinding sideways and burning rubber tracks. Andrew looked in the direction they were bound, the motorway's concrete supports were getting bigger, fast. He remembered Mona's warning. He closed his eyes. But when he opened them he was still alive. The car had stopped. It rocked back and forth on its suspension a few times before settling. Jones said an expletive.

They had revolved and were facing the slip road. In the headlights was Blondie, slumped against the barrier and licking her wounds. They realised it was not oil the car had skidded on. It was Blondie's blood. Twice she caught up with twenty-nine and twice it threw her off, easily. She could do no more. Twenty-nine was bounding along the motorway towards Black Mountain. Nothing was going to stop it finding May.

34

May crept into the dormitory. Mona was asleep, one pillow under her head and another hugged tight to her face. May sat on the edge of Mona's bed.

'Mona, wake up.' She gave her a soft shake.

Mona rubbed her eyes. 'It's too early for breakfast,' she said.

'I know,' said May, 'ye can go back to sleep in a minute. I just wanted to say I'm sorry for being spiteful.'

Mona absorbed the apology sleepily.

'Though I wouldn't really have told about your Talent,' May went on, 'I'd have stopped.'

'No, you wouldn't have stopped,' Mona said. 'You would have told, totally.'

'I—' May bit her lip.

'But that's okay,' said Mona. 'I'll forgive you if you promise never to tell.'

'Never,' said May emphatically. She felt around, seeking Mona's hand. Mona spread her fingers and their hands locked together.

'Okay,' said Mona.

'Never ever,' said May.

'Okay.'

'Never ever ever.'

'I'm going back to sleep now,' said Mona.

May pulled off her boots and fell onto her bed. Sleep crept warmly over her. Her eyes were closed exactly four seconds when Lizzy Gamble started screaming.

Everyone woke. Lizzy was up on her bed, backed against the headboard. One hand was around her throat and the other flapping towards May.

'MAY,' she screamed. 'THE DOG GOT MAY.'

Lizzy rolled to the floor and crawled away fast. At the wall beneath the window she kept crawling. She slammed into the wall face first and flopped. The girls gathered around her. Rosy gently took her head in both hands.

'What was she going on about?' asked Sally. ' "Got May"?'

'Why'd she go straight into the wall?' demanded Tara.

May stood at the end of her bed. She looked at Lizzy. She looked at the wall. The wall seemed to stretch up and up. Or was it that she was sinking?

'Because,' said May, 'in one minute the wall won't be there any more.'

Pandemonium. The girls surged around the room.

Tara bellowed for Elizabeth, her bed was next to the condemned wall. She and Sally lifted her, dropped her in the wheelchair and pushed her towards the door. Rosy dragged Lizzy out. The impossibility of May's situation left her standing. She knew how the dogs worked. One had her scent. Where could she run? Nowhere.

Along the motorway came a beat only May could hear.

Tara and Sally heaved Elizabeth upstairs. The rest of the girls clambered after them. May could hear the nun's footsteps through the ceiling. Then Sister Perpetua's voice, 'Girls, what's the meaning of this?'

WEARE WEARE WEARE WEARE WEARE . . .

Outside, a bark broke the dawn silence. It also broke four windows.

Mona ran back into the dormitory, grabbed May by the wrist and pulled her upstairs. They headed for Sister Primrose's door but Tara stepped in May's way. May bounced off her and landed on her back.

'It's you it's after,' said Tara. 'Stay away from us.'

The building buckled. Everyone was thrown sideways. Walls, floors and ceilings twisted towards each other and sat at new and severe angles. From the floor May watched as, in rapid succession, each thread of the stairs bent upwards and snapped. Then Sister Perpetua was pulling May into her chamber.

'I'll get you away,' she said.

WEARE WEARE WEARE WEARE WEARE . . .

Floorboards parted as the house bent. The girls pressed themselves in a corner of Sister Primrose's room. Through the floor they saw the head and back of the creature, sniffing and digging across the hall and into the common room.

Sister Perpetua pushed May ahead out the window. They dropped to the roof of the stable. Saint was kicking his stable door, desperate to escape. May would have felt the horse's terror but for the hammer of the Furies pulverising everything. The dog turned to the back of the house and the upper level rippled over its spine. Elizabeth was thrown upwards. When she landed there was no floor. She fell to the common room. The wheels of her chair compressed into ovals before flopping sideways. Elizabeth was left lying on the carpet between the dog's front paws. She was smiling.

Twenty-nine's head swung back around to the offering. She was not the object of the chase but the Furies were drawn to her. Above, Sister Primrose and Sally held Tara from jumping down.

We are . . . We are . . . We are . . . We are . . . We are . . . We are . . .

May gasped and looked towards where, beyond the walls and inside the dog, the Furies were cooling. Even they were not immune to Elizabeth's power. Twenty-nine sniffed at her curiously.

You ... are? ... You are? ... You ...? ... are? ...
You? ... You ... are? ...

The beat of the Furies was breaking down. They were confused by an encounter with their opposite. At that moment May realised the Furies were more than an infestation. They had a kind of intelligence. They regarded Elizabeth as a puzzle.

you are you ... you are you ...

But was she a puzzle worth solving?

we are what we are ...

you are what you are ...

we are what we are ... and we are ...

we are monster ...

Sister Perpetua seized Saint's mane before he bolted. 'Saint will get you away from here,' she said. She grabbed May's waist and hoisted her up. There was no saddle. No reins.

'I don't know how!' shouted May.

'Just hang on!'

Sister Perpetua knotted May's fingers into Saint's mane and pressed her knee against his side. Then she let him go.

we are monster ... We Are Monster ...
WeAreMonster ... WeAre ... WeAre ...

Twenty-nine turned from Elizabeth. May's scent, laden with fresh fear, electrified the Furies again.

WEARE WEARE WEARE ...

Twenty-nine lowered its head and charged the wall.

A wave of bricks splashed over the grounds and the dog was out. Even with its bad eyesight it could see May galloping up the mountain. The Furies pumped like petrol in twenty-nine's black and broken veins. It barked with joy. The chase was back on.

35

May was chucked about until she slotted into rhythm with Saint's stride and instead of bouncing against him she rode with him. Having broken away from the Furies she could feel Saint's fear. It was equal to her own.

May thought the trees were the best way to go. But how to steer Saint? Then he swerved towards them of his own accord. May ducked. Branches whizzed overhead.

Smart horse, she thought. *The trees will slow the dog*.

But not by much. Behind her, May heard trees bowled aside. Roots ripped, trunks spread and fell. The whole forest shook. May glimpsed the blasted oak. Its black stumps were revealed against a dawn-tinted sky. Saint galloped a tight path through the trees while dog-driven disaster raged after. Saint knew the way. A stone wall marked the edge of the trees. He had jumped it many times.

Saint left the ground and everything went quiet. May

felt the windy sensation of flight. Three seconds later Saint met the ground and went straight into a gallop. They aimed for the field's far wall. May dared to look behind. No sign of the dog but she saw treetops rocking apart. She faced forwards again as Saint left the ground. This flight ended with a bone-jarring thump and the stony clatter of hooves. They had hit the hard surface of a lane. Saint turned up Black Mountain just as twenty-nine crashed through the wall by the trees.

Something strange happened. Ravens swooped and attacked the dog. They jostled its eyes and pecked hard at its muzzle. The dog's outsized jaws snapped at them, tossing broken birds over its back. The ravens wheeled around and assaulted again but they could not stop the giant. The dog shook them off.

The lane wound up Black Mountain. Saint's lungs heaved in and out between May's legs. He was tiring beneath her, his rhythm slowing. May glanced back. The lane was clear. She clutched at the possibility they had lost the dog. Then a length of stone wall exploded outwards and the dog swung onto the lane. It was gaining.

Best to head across country, thought May.

Behind them something new joined the chase. The high beam of car headlights flooded up the lane.

Saint decided to jump a wall and head across country. He leaped. It was not like flight this time. It was the leaden sensation of gravity winning.

Crack.

A fetlock struck the top of the wall. Saint landed awkwardly, legs kicking independently of each other for a few seconds before finding rhythm. Twenty-nine charged the wall. Boulders flew across the field as if they were pebbles. May and Saint's terror mingled, neither knew the difference. *I'm sorry*, May thought. Then Saint was whipped from under her.

Twenty-nine's teeth had caught Saint's flank. The horse snapped back while May's momentum threw her over his head. She spun through the air, hit the field and kept rolling. When she stopped she was on her back looking at stars. From underneath her skull she felt the disinterest of earthworms. Where was Saint's fear, the thing filling her mind until a second ago?

It was gone. Extinguished.

Saint still looked graceful as he flew through the air three metres above her. His hooves seemed to step along the sky. But Saint's torso was a ripped sack, streaming intestines and shredded muscle. From where May lay, drops of Saint's blood left a trail across the sky. Until it fell upon her, as red rain.

Twenty-nine careered right past May. Turning sharply, it hit the far wall side on and collapsed it. Then something new entered the field. It screeched off the lane and rode rough over the broken wall. It was all sparks and lights. The car came to a shaking stop close to May.

'Do you have your gun?' Ewan asked hopefully.

'No, I'm not on duty,' Jones said.

The car was still shuddering. They saw that May was backing away.

'She doesn't want to draw it to us,' said Ewan.

Why was the car *still* shuddering?

Both Ewan and Jones whipped around and looked at Andrew. They had forgotten he was there.

Andrew stared at them with yellow eyes. The last syringe of the Furies was drained, it fell from his fingers and lay between his shoes. Andrew's feet were no longer in his shoes. They had burst out. As they watched his arms bulged and elongated. His watch strap snapped. His hair stood on end. His teeth stretched in his jawbone as his jawbone stretched in his head. The Furies were exploring Andrew's body. They liked it.

Andrew lunged for the door. Unable to get his fingers around the handle he kicked it. The door shot off and skimmed across the field.

Andrew tugged himself from the car and stood facing twenty-nine. The dog, crouched at the far end of the field, bared its teeth. Andrew bared his. He went for the car door lying on the grass. He arrived at it so quickly it confused him. Its lightness confused him too. He held it up in one hand. He heard May speaking to him but could not grasp the meaning of words. But Andrew knew who she was. He knew who he was. He was going to defend May from the dog.

Andrew, or the half-monster that once was Andrew, threw the car door like a Frisbee. It spun at the dog. May felt the beat of the Furies in twenty-nine waver; for a split second the mentality of their dog host asserted itself. The dog jumped and snatched the door out of the air. It seemed that somewhere, deep down, twenty-nine was still an ordinary dog. Andrew looked at the rocks blasted from the broken wall and strewn around him. Somewhere, not quite so deep, he still had Andrew's grasp of tactics.

The dog crunched and the car door went to pieces. The sensation of breakage in its mouth drove the dog back into the grip of the Furies. The smell of May, her sweat and tears, it had to taste them. It charged.

Andrew stepped into twenty-nine's path. He picked up a rock the size of a car tyre. Andrew's wrist strained slightly as he judged its weight.

TooBig

Andrew dropped the rock and took a smaller one. It felt good loaded on the end of his arm. The thudding footfalls of the dog only helped Andrew focus. He threw the rock straight as a laser beam.

Twenty-nine jumped into the path of the missile with its jaws open. But the rock was too fast to catch. It shot into twenty-nine's mouth, knocked the tips off its teeth, then barrelled down its throat. The rock's trajectory blasted it out the back of the dog's skull. Slick with gore, the rock bounced down the field and away.

Despite its punctured head the dog made two more bounds before faltering. Its chin smacked the ground but it drove on, ploughing a channel in the field. When it finally came to a halt its nose was by Andrew's feet. Its tongue unrolled and lay twitching.

Only when the dog was fully dead were Andrew's Furies satisfied. He grunted. He tried to fold his arms but found he could not, one was bigger than the other. His arteries were thick black cords under the skin. He looked at his forearms, trying to work out what was wrong. His mind seemed dulled but he was not sure, he could not remember how it was before. He was certain of one thing. He had given his life away.

Andrew stood against the sky and howled.

36

Akeem spent days in the white corridors and waiting rooms of officialdom. The port authority questioned the crew of the *Bounder*. They had a story and they were sticking to it. An explosion in the cargo had breached the hull. Not so unlikely, the cargo belonged to a man charged with several murders. The pumps malfunctioned and they were unable to keep the freighter afloat. At 3.30 am the captain decided to abandon ship.

'Best to keep things simple,' Captain Marcus whispered to Akeem. No one was near but something about this place made whispering seem wise. They were sitting side by side in a corridor, waiting. Occasionally a civil servant bustled past. They all looked the same to Akeem except some were men and some were ladies. They seemed to be carrying the same folder back and forth.

'I am sorry you lost your boat,' said Akeem.

In reply Captain Marcus pulled up one trouser leg.

His leg ended just below the knee. The rest was polished plastic and gleaming chrome. Captain Marcus took pride in his appearance and had learned to accept the prosthetic leg as an accessory, like a pair of dark glasses. He even liked the plastic's cream colour. The leg was originally made for a white man but this suited Captain Marcus fine. He knew no boundaries. He was a man of the world.

'I was like you when I was a boy,' said Captain Marcus. 'Loved to wander. Except I built my own boats instead of hiding in other people's.' He laughed and nudged Akeem with his elbow. 'Our village was on a river and I built rafts to travel it. One day I went miles too far. I had to abandon my raft and walk home. While walking I saw a shiny metal thing in the ground. I thought it might be a useful part for my next raft so I poked at it with my toe to find out what it was.'

Akeem frowned at the leg.

'Landmines still function *years* after being planted,' explained Captain Marcus. 'In a way, they are targeted at boys, boys like us. Because we are curious. If we see a shiny thing in the ground we want to know what it is. If I had bent down to pick it up I would be dead. Instead . . .' He rapped his leg with his knuckle. 'Somebody made the landmine. Somebody planted it. In between somebody sold and transported it. It took a lot of people to take away my leg.'

They waited some more.

'Besides,' Captain Marcus added, 'the *Bounder* was insured.'

Akeem smiled at that. He had been insured too, by God himself. It still overwhelmed Akeem to remember the seals. He would never see Andrew, May or Ewan again. He knew nothing about them, apart from their first names. Their memory would fade but Akeem would never forget God's intervention.

'I already know of another coaster for sale,' said Captain Marcus. 'It awaits our inspection in Lagos.'

'I was only away two weeks in the end,' said Akeem.

'It is not too late to ask to stay here,' Captain Marcus reminded him. 'We can tell them I have never seen you before.'

'No, this way is best,' said Akeem.

The door opened and Mr Port Authority called them into his office. He opened a folder and read with glasses perched on his nose. 'We're happy to help with your repatriation,' he said. 'We've had plane tickets issued. As the boy does not have a passport we've arranged an emergency visa. I suggest you don't take him on international trips without documentation in future.'

Captain Marcus nodded solemnly. He was not used to being told what to do.

'Unusual, if may I say so,' said Mr Port Authority as he walked with them out of the building and into the sun, 'a Christian man with a Muslim son. Was it an adoption?'

'Yes it was,' Captain Marcus said proudly. He put his arm around Akeem.

'But do not let appearances fool you,' said Akeem. 'It was I who adopted him.'

37

Ewan met Jones on the bitumen path. The grass grew lime-juice green. The sprinklers sprinkled. Ewan was returning from his mother's grave.

'I regret not asking her about things,' said Ewan as they walked.

'What kind of things, hmm?'

'Like, what it was like for her when she was fourteen,' said Ewan. After a few moments he added decisively, 'I should have asked her more questions.'

The sprinklers were the only sound for a while.

'There was another sighting of your dog in the mountains,' said Jones. 'I'm sure it'll be captured soon.'

'I don't think Blondie is any danger,' said Ewan. 'Not any more. But are you honestly glad I didn't set her on my father?'

'Yes I am,' replied Jones.

'I am not so sure.'

'Keep your heart for the love and your head for the hate,' said Jones.

Ewan was glad Jones knew about the hate. It was a real thing. No good smoothing over it. 'What do you mean?' he asked.

'We shouldn't control love,' she said. 'I told Stirling that a few times, that we shouldn't think about it too hard. So the heart is for storing it. But hate must be controlled. So the head is for storing that. Watch the hate or it'll cause havoc. He never will again, but Franklin created victims. If you'd set the dog on him you'd just be another. Another person defined by what happened to them instead of what they did. You're not a victim. What are you instead?'

Ewan thought about it. 'A survivor,' he said eventually.

Jones smiled. 'That's your head working,' she said.

Parked outside the graveyard was Jones's car. They could already hear Andrew snoring in the back seat.

38

Andrew had problems. He was separated from other people. It was like he was in a glass box, glass as thick as a shark tank. Slowly he realised the doctors and nurses could not understand him. They replied to each other's noises but not his. When he made his noises he saw confusion in their faces. Sometimes he saw fear. Now Andrew understood people best by the light of their eyes and the touch of their hands. Andrew's grasp of language was slipping. Language was history.

They passed his body through machines. Ran tubes into his arms. What was going on? He just wanted to know what was going on. He grabbed people sometimes and had to be restrained.

He got lots of attention. There were his parents, grieving. There was Ewan, reading to him from books. There were the doctors, telling visitors not to hold his hand. There was May, holding it anyway.

It was the smaller hand she held.

Mona Longley was not exactly right. Andrew's life

had not ended, but he was no longer alive in the same way. Andrew knew that he was missing something but he did not know what. This unnameable loss frustrated him. That morning he had punched a hole in the wall of his hospital room. Ewan calmed him. Ewan and Jones took him for a drive.

Andrew was host to the Furies. Unnatural strength was wound tight inside him. His gums ached with enlarged teeth. His heartbeat could be heard two metres away. His hands were powerful but no longer capable of delicate work. Clots of the Furies had fused to his spinal cord and brain, they whispered directly into his neural pathways. His bones were stretched, his flesh was pumped, his dreams were violent and frightful.

Ewan had led him towards the car park. The nurses were glad of a break. They shivered when Andrew tried to smile at them. They did not think Andrew could be cured. Ewan feared they were right.

One person would try to prove them wrong. It was her mission.

39

May looked at the ravens flying the high air. Beneath, a wide swathe of flattened trunks divided the trees. She was standing a safe distance from the crooked hulk of the school. It creaked in the breeze, shifting its weight from one wall to another. Yellow tape was wrapped around it, as if attempting to hold it together. Along the tape's length was repeated, 'Condemned Building. Do Not Enter'.

Most of the students had been sent home to their families. Mona and Rafferty were going on a trip with Sister Perpetua.

'You'll come back when the school's rebuilt, won't you?' Mona asked her.

'I'd *like* to,' May said, 'but this thing with Andrew, I don't know where it will take us.'

'We certainly hope to keep you,' Sister Perpetua said as she approached.

May tried to hide her shock at the change in Sister Perpetua. The nun was noticeably shrunken. She walked slowly and carefully over the gravel as if a new delicacy etched her bones.

'We'll have a shorter title when we reopen,' Sister Perpetua said. 'The Black Mountain School for Gifted Girls.'

'You're goin' to take all sorts!' said May.

Sister Perpetua smiled, her lips were definitely thinner. 'We've been taking all sorts already.'

'Ye found out about—?' May began to say but stopped and glanced to Mona.

'It wasn't as big a secret as Rosy thought,' said Sister Perpetua. 'This school was never only Catholic. But in this part of the world we have been drawing lines for years. It gets so you explain away exceptions rather than let them shake your beliefs. The church position was that the institution of the Gifts was Catholic even if sometimes the Gifts were bestowed on others. Rafferty's not a Catholic either.'

'Or Lizzy,' Mona chipped in.

May laughed at the revelations. But that was only the beginning. Something tugged at her mind. She forgot everything and ran to the back of the school. Parked there was the school's little car, an open horse-box clasped to the tow bar. Rafferty was leading a horse towards it.

'Saint!' May said, not believing.

Was this a black ghost? She had seen Saint mortally wounded. May touched his side. A knobby scar ran from his shoulder around the curve of his belly and on to his hindquarters. Saint was somehow resealed.

May turned to Sister Perpetua. 'What's your Talent?' she asked.

'My fingers can weld tissue together,' said Sister Perpetua. She ran her fingers hard along the scar in Saint's side. May thought she saw blue energy crackle from her fingertips but when she blinked it was gone.

'I discovered my Gift young,' said Sister Perpetua. 'But had only used it twice before. Using the power cost me a lot. It stunted my growth.'

'Ye used it again to fix Saint,' May said.

'Yes, it took hours. All the girls came up and assisted me. The intestines were complicated.'

May understood Sister Perpetua's sudden aging. 'I'm sorry for bringing ye all this trouble,' she said.

'It wasn't your fault,' Sister Perpetua said, stroking Saint's nose, 'and I would do it again. It gives me great satisfaction. I was envious of your ability to tap into Saint but now I have too.'

Rafferty spoke. 'When Sister Perpetua was working on Saint, myself and some of the others got shovels and buried the remains of that creature. A couple of hours after dying its body was all flat, like a balloon with all the air out of it. The grass was brown. Sally says the rupture around the site was the worse she ever felt. She says the parasites inside the dog are not dead. They had only wriggled out of the dog and gone into the ground. So, they're still there, in the land.'

'Hopefully they'll stay deep,' said May.

'Nightmare,' said Mona. 'I hope the land recovers.'

'It'll take years,' said Rafferty. She wondered if she would be the only one around long enough to see it.

They heard a car coming up the driveway. It was Jones bringing Ewan and Andrew.

'We're goin' to find a cure for Andrew,' May said.

Sister Perpetua nodded. She looked at her hands. 'I'm sorry my fingers can do nothing for his infection. But I'll pray for you both. Yours is a good mission.'

'Aye,' May said, 'it's the only important thing.'

Then something happened. It happened not because May wanted it but because she needed it. Because the time was right. A bird swooped down and perched on her shoulder. The sudden weight of it caused May to stagger forward. Turning her head she looked into its dark eye. It was the raven, unable to resist May's newly expanded Talent. It wanted her approval. There was something in its beak. The raven dropped the burnt acorn into the palm of May's hand.